Pet Finders Club

Runaway Rascal

by Ben M. Baglio

Cover art by Andrew Beckett
Interior art by Meg Aubrey

SCHOLASTIC INC.

New York   Toronto   London   Auckland   Sydney
Mexico City   New Delhi   Hong Kong   Buenos Aires

Special thanks to Lucy Courtenay

ISBN 0-439-79250-9

12 11 10 9 8 7 6 5 4 3 2 1   6 7 8 9 10 11/0

Printed in the U.S.A.
First Scholastic printing, March 2006

Chapter One

Andi Talbot frowned at her open suitcase. She was sure she'd packed only one sweater so far, and suddenly there were three.

She looked at the little tan-and-white terrier lying at the end of her bed. "Did you put these in here, Buddy?" she asked.

The terrier pricked up his ears before settling his head back on his paws. Andi reached over to rub his neck.

"Mom?" she called. "Did you put all these extra sweaters in my suitcase?"

"It's only March, Andi," Judy Talbot said, coming into the room. "This is Washington State, not Florida, remember? You'll need those sweaters when you're staying with the Saunderses. The forecast is wet and cold this week."

Andi sighed. She preferred the hot Florida weather, where she and her mom used to live. A wet forecast for Spring Break was one of the downsides of living near Seattle.

"Oh, and don't forget to pack enough socks," her mom added, "or you might wind up borrowing a pair of Tristan's."

"Ew." Andi shuddered.

"You *are* okay about me going to this conference, aren't you?" Judy Talbot asked anxiously. "It's only for a week."

"Quit worrying, Mom," Andi said, heading for the bathroom to get her toothbrush. "We'll have a great time."

Although she was going to miss her mom, Andi was really looking forward to staying with Tristan Saunders. He and Natalie Lewis were her two best friends in Orchard Park. They'd set up the Pet Finders Club when Andi had first moved here, after she'd lost Buddy for a few days.

"I know you might have preferred to stay with Natalie, but it just wasn't possible this week," her mom continued as Andi returned with her toothbrush. "They've got their hands full with the party, not to mention their houseguest — Marissa?"

"Melissa," Andi corrected, tucking her toothbrush into her suitcase.

"Pretty name," said Mrs. Talbot. "Is Natalie getting along with her?"

Natalie hadn't sounded very excited about her guest when Andi had spoken to her the night before. But Andi didn't want to sound unkind. "I think they're . . . pretty different," she said.

"Oh, well," Mrs. Talbot said diplomatically. "At least they've got the party to look forward to."

Natalie's stepdad was turning forty at the end of the week and, according to Natalie, her mom was planning the party of the century. She had shared every detail of the plans with Andi: the jazz band with their white tuxedos and gold bow ties, the Thai-style appetizers, and, most important, Natalie's pale blue beaded outfit and her mom's red satin gown.

Just before she took her suitcase downstairs, Andi managed to sneak out one of the sweaters and replace it with her favorite hoodie. She added a couple more books and tossed in an extra CD. Then she closed the lid and carried it down, with Buddy close at her heels.

It was only a five-minute drive to the Saunderses' house, where Tristan, his parents, and his brother,

Dean, were waiting for them. After Andi had said good-bye to her mom (and promised to wear a sweater at least once that week), the whole family, Andi, and Buddy headed inside.

"It's really kind of you to have me *and* Bud, Mrs. Saunders," Andi said gratefully. "Are you sure Lucy's going to be okay having Buddy around?"

Mrs. Saunders smiled. "Lucy's a pretty sassy cat," she said. "If Buddy doesn't watch it, Lucy'll put him in his place."

Andi put Buddy in the backyard, where he started happily sniffing his way around the flower beds. The sky was beginning to look gray and threatening, and Andi knew they'd have rain before long.

"Dean's making pizza for lunch, but that won't be for ages," Tristan explained. "Do you want to try my new computer game? I'm already pretty good at it," he added, "so don't worry if you don't win, like, ever."

"Gee, you're really convincing," Andi told him.

"I think Andi might prefer to unpack first," Mrs. Saunders suggested. "She's here all week, Tristan. The game can wait."

"This is where you'll be staying," Mrs. Saunders announced, leading the way upstairs and opening a door across the landing from Tristan's room.

"I'm sorry we can't stay and help you settle in," Mrs. Saunders apologized. "There's a new development on the east side of Orchard Park that we have to take a look at this morning. Enjoy your pizza!"

Tristan's parents ran a real estate business and when they weren't at home, Tristan's older brother, Dean, took charge. He was an excellent cook, if a little experimental. Andi wondered nervously what the pizza options would be.

After Tristan's parents had left, Andi looked around for Tristan's cat. "Where's Lucy?"

"On a beautiful morning like this?" Tristan said, heading into the kitchen. Outside, the sky was looking increasingly dark and ominous. "Where any self-respecting cat would be: on my bed. Listen, Andi, I don't think Luce is looking forward to seeing Buddy," he warned. "She's been sharpening her claws ever since I told her you and Bud were coming to visit."

"Your mom thinks they'll be fine," said Andi. "Buddy likes cats."

"Sure he does," Tristan said, "between two slices of bread."

He was very protective of his beautiful silver tabby, Lucy, who had been missing for several months before the Pet Finders Club had tracked her down.

"Buddy only really chased Lucy once before," Andi pointed out.

Tristan looked unconvinced. "Lucy sleeps in the kitchen at night," he said. "I thought we could put Buddy in the utility room so we can shut the door."

"Relax," Andi told him. "Bud's got a whole new environment to sniff and a new yard to run around in. The last thing on his mind will be chasing Lucy." She wasn't totally convinced that this was true, but she didn't want to worry Tristan. Opening the back door, she called, "Buddy! Here, boy!"

Buddy raced inside and went straight for Lucy's cat bed, which was tucked in a cozy corner of the kitchen. He sniffed it with interest and gave a little yip. On cue, Lucy came into the kitchen, her soft paws making no noise on the tiled floor. Tristan went to scoop her up, but Andi laid her hand on his arm.

"Let's see what happens," she suggested.

Lucy stopped when she saw Buddy and looked like she was going to take a step back. Then she hissed. Buddy cocked his head and pricked up his ears. *Please don't chase her*, Andi prayed, ready to grab the terrier by the scruff of the neck if he made a move.

After staring at each other for a couple of seconds, Lucy hissed again. Then she padded closer and sniffed at Buddy's nose. Buddy tried to lick her, but Lucy's paw shot out and cuffed him around the ear. Her claws weren't out, but Buddy looked quite shocked! He promptly lay down and rolled onto his back, as if he wanted to make friends. Lucy gave him a withering look from her beautiful blue eyes, then stalked past him and took a drink from her water bowl.

"Bad luck, Bud," Andi said. "I'm sure she'll get used to you." Beside her, Tristan looked very relieved.

The doorbell buzzed, and Tristan went to open the door, with Andi and Buddy following close behind. Natalie, her black Labrador, Jet, and a girl Andi had never seen before stood on the porch. Above their heads, there was a rumble of thunder, and rain began pattering on the slate roof of the porch. Andi bent down and picked up Buddy, remembering how it was a storm that had frightened him into running away when they first moved to Orchard Park.

"Jet is totally off-the-wall today," Natalie said as her excitable dog tried to jump up at everyone on the porch. "This is Melissa, guys," she added, waving her hand at the girl standing next to her. "Melissa, this is Andi and Tristan, and Andi's dog, Buddy. My mom and Melissa's mom go way back, blah blah. Thanks for the invitation to lunch, by the way. Pizza's my favorite."

When Natalie stopped to breathe, Melissa smiled shyly. She had blond hair with shaggy bangs that hung around her small heart-shaped face, and she was wearing jeans and a blue baseball jacket. The way she tilted her head to one side reminded Andi of a little bird.

"Oh, I almost forgot!" Natalie squeaked, delving in her purse and pulling out two long, cream-colored envelopes. "Here's your invitation to the party, Tris, and yours, too, Andi. Don't they look great?"

Tristan tore open his envelope. "You are invited to a birthday celebration," he read aloud from the thick, creamy card. Overhearing, Dean came out of the kitchen to check out the invitation and introduced himself to Melissa with a smile.

"I wanted Mom to send us one," Natalie said earnestly, "but she said no."

"You wanted an invitation to your own party?" Tristan said in surprise.

"It's so exciting when you get invitations in the mail," Natalie explained. "It's better than all the boring stuff that usually comes. No one ever sends me anything."

"Except Neil," Melissa piped up. "Ouch!" She exclaimed suddenly. "What was that for?"

Natalie turned bright pink as she pulled her foot back from having stepped on Melissa's toe. Tristan and Andi looked at her questioningly.

"Neil?" Andi echoed. "Would that be Neil O'Connor, from Hollow Creek Riding Center? How come he's sending you mail?"

Neil's mom ran a riding center outside Orchard Park, where Andi and Natalie had been taking Western-style lessons.

Natalie tossed her hair back. "It was just a postcard," she said. "He's staying with his cousins in Wyoming for a few days. No big deal."

Tristan's eyebrows shot up. "A postcard from your boyfriend? That sounds like a big deal to me."

"He's not my boyfriend!"

"You said he was this morning," Melissa said, looking puzzled.

"I did *not*," Natalie said. "You misunderstood." Looking flustered, she bent down to take off Jet's leash. Jet promptly leaped away from her and chased Buddy into the kitchen.

"Sorry I had to bring Melissa along," Natalie whispered to Andi as they ran into the kitchen after the two dogs. "Mom sprung her on me this week. Her parents have gone to Europe, but Melissa didn't want to go, so her mom thought it would be fun for her to spend Spring Break in Seattle. I don't know why."

Andi glanced back down the hall where Tristan and Dean were talking to Melissa. She was laughing at something Tristan had said. "She seems nice," Andi said.

"She's okay." Natalie shrugged. "We don't know each other that well. I mean, we meet a couple of times a year when our folks get together, but that's all."

There was a volley of barking and the sound of claws scrabbling from the utility room, followed by a spitting noise. Jet yelped. Moments later, a Lucy-shaped blur streaked past Andi and Natalie and straight up the stairs. Buddy and Jet sauntered back into the kitchen then. They flopped down on the tiled floor with their tongues hanging out, so the girls left them in there.

"Sounds like Lucy straightened Jet out," Andi joked as they made their way back into the hall. "She's got her paws full today, with both those dogs."

"Catch you guys later," Dean said, heading past in the other direction. "Lunch will be ready in about an hour."

"Let's go into the den," Tristan suggested. "The dogs can come in there."

"It'll be a pet party." Andi grinned.

"That would be my perfect party," Melissa said enthusiastically.

Andi was pleased. It sounded like she and Melissa had something in common. "Do you have any pets, Melissa?"

"I have a dwarf rabbit," she replied, her face lighting up. "Her name's Rascal."

"And is she?" Tristan asked. "A rascal, I mean?"

"She's already tried to eat my new satin slippers," Natalie grumbled, joining Andi on the squishy couch beneath the window.

"You brought Rascal to Orchard Park?" Andi asked Melissa in surprise.

Melissa nodded. "Rascal's pretty tense, and she gets really unhappy without me," she said. "This one time, we tried a petsitter, but Rascal totally freaked out. It took ages to get her back into her usual routine. So, I thought I'd bring her with me. It took a while to persuade Mom and Dad, but Natalie's parents were really nice and said it would be okay. It's only a half-hour drive from home, and she sat on my lap in her carry case the whole time. She was really good."

"And now she's running around my bedroom eating my stuff." Natalie sighed.

"She didn't eat your slippers," Melissa said. "She just sniffed them a little."

"She sniffed them with her *teeth*," Natalie corrected

her. When Melissa looked upset, she added quickly, "But she is pretty cute, I guess."

"She's the softest thing you've ever felt," Melissa said dreamily. "Honestly, sometimes I stroke her and it's like I can hardly even feel her fur. She's an indoor rabbit, so she's house-trained and everything. She's the best pet in the world."

Andi thought of the comforting roughness of Buddy's coat. It sounded like having a rabbit would be a totally different experience. "I'd love to meet Rascal," she said.

She was about to ask if they could come and see the rabbit sometime that week when her cell phone started ringing. Andi fished it out of her pocket. "Hello?"

Her mom's voice crackled into her ear. "I just got to the airport, honey," she said. "I thought I'd check to be sure you're settling in okay. Did you offer to help Mrs. Saunders with dinner tonight, like we discussed?"

"I didn't get a chance yet," Andi said, shifting the phone to her other ear and glancing apologetically at the others.

"Well, don't forget," Mrs. Talbot continued. "It's hard work having guests. Is your room nice?"

"Mom, can we talk about this later?"

"Oh, okay," her mom said, feigning disappointment.

"Bye, Mom." She turned back to Melissa once she'd

hung up. "I was going to ask if we could come by and see Rascal — "

Her phone started ringing again. Impatiently, Andi clicked it on. "Mom, I really can't talk now," she began.

"Uh, hello?" said a boy's voice. He sounded close to tears. "Is this the Pet Finders Club?"

Andi moved to the edge of the couch, instantly alert. "Yes?"

"I saw your flyer on a telephone pole near my house," said the boy. "My name's Will Jacobs. It's about my cat, Tiger. He's disappeared. Please say you'll find him. Please!"

Chapter Two

Andi covered the mouthpiece of the phone with her hand and hissed, "Tris, Nat, we've got a missing cat named Tiger. Get me some paper, quick!"

Tristan produced a pad of paper from a table at the side of the room while Natalie took a pen out of her purse.

Andi tucked the phone more securely under her chin. "What's your address, Will?" She scribbled it down. "We'll be over in ten minutes," she promised and hung up.

Melissa looked confused. "What was all that about? Over where?"

"Two four two five Oakley Avenue," Andi read. "That's only four blocks away."

Tristan had retrieved his backpack from the hall and was peering inside.

"Notebook?" Natalie said. "Pencil? Plastic wallet for photographs?"

"Check, check, and check," Tristan said, flipping the backpack closed again.

"What's this about a missing cat? Why are we going to this place?" Melissa asked, following Andi and the others as they shut the dogs in the utility room and started putting on their coats.

"It's our Pet Finders Club," Natalie explained. "I told you about it, remember? The call Andi took was from a boy who's lost his cat, so we're going over to ask him questions that might help find it: when it went missing, what it looks like, stuff like that."

"But it's lunch in an hour," Melissa pointed out. "Can't it wait?"

Tristan stopped in his tracks. "Good point. Hey, Deano!" he called through the kitchen door. "We have to make a PFC call, okay? Can lunch wait?"

"I didn't mean lunch," Melissa began.

Dean appeared at the kitchen door. "Sure," he said, drying his hands on his black-and-white-checked apron. "See you around two."

"Two o'clock?" Melissa said in dismay. "But that means we won't be back at your place until after three, Natalie. I have to feed Rascal at two o'clock."

"The Pet Finders Club always comes first with us, Melissa," Andi explained gently. "We drop whatever we're doing and go look for the missing pet. Every minute is vital."

"This may not take much time," Tristan added. "We could still make it back for pizza and get to Nat's place in time to feed Rascal."

Melissa looked unconvinced.

"Let's see how it goes," Natalie said. "If we have to leave early to feed Rascal, we will. Tristan and Andi can come over this afternoon with some leftover pizza and tell me anything I missed. Okay?"

"And meet Rascal," Andi added.

"Awesome," Melissa said, looking a little happier. She took down her coat from the hook in the hall, but then gasped as she looked out of the window. Sheets of rain were hammering down. "It's really wet out there," she said. "Do we really have to do this?"

"It's just a little shower," Natalie said, raising her voice over the furious drumming on the windows. "You're going to love pet finding, Melissa. It's all part of the Orchard Park experience!"

Tristan found three umbrellas on the porch, and they set out like a trio of brightly colored mushrooms. Melissa was wearing new high-tops, but she stepped around the worst puddles and didn't complain. Andi tucked her hand into the crook of her elbow to share the umbrella. When she gave Melissa a grin, she was relieved to see Melissa grin back.

The Jacobses' house was set a little way back from the road. There were three steps up to the front door and a freshly painted white wooden porch, where Will Jacobs was waiting for them. He was an anxious-looking boy of about twelve, with a thin face and very dark brown eyes.

"Thanks for coming," he said.

"No problem," Andi replied as they shook out their umbrellas and stood them neatly on the porch. "I'm Andi, and these are my friends Tristan, Natalie, and Melissa."

Will hung up their coats and led them into a large, airy kitchen, where they all sat around a wooden table.

Tristan pulled out his notebook and opened it to a fresh page. "Okay, Will. What can you tell us?"

"Where should I start?" Will asked anxiously.

"Tell us exactly when you noticed Tiger was missing," Andi suggested.

"He didn't come home two nights ago," Will said, "which was pretty unusual, but Tiger's an independent cat. We looked around the neighborhood yesterday, but we didn't want to report it in case he came back on his own. When he didn't come back last night, Mom told me to call you."

"Is your mom home?" Andi asked.

Will shook his head. "She had to go out. Dad's working now, but he'll be back later."

"Can you tell us what Tiger looks like?" Natalie prompted.

Will clasped his hands around his knees. "He's a fat tabby cat with awesome gold and chocolate stripes and a white tummy."

"Does he have a collar?" Andi said.

Will shook his head. "We tried to get him to wear one, but Tiger hated it and used to pull it off."

Tristan made a note.

"What's he like?" Natalie asked. "I mean, character-wise?"

"He's really affectionate. . . ." Will stopped, and started picking at a frayed patch on his jeans. Andi noticed that his eyes looked a little wet. He cleared his throat and started again. "He's really affectionate and sociable, but he loves hunting outside on his own, too. Like I said, he's pretty independent, but he always comes back at night."

"You say he's been gone for two days?" Andi checked. Will nodded. "Is it unusual for him to miss his meals?"

Will shook his head. "Not really. He's picky with his food and doesn't always eat everything on his plate, even though he's not exactly underweight. Actually, he's pretty heavy. I can't hold him for long without my arms starting to ache. His favorite food's sardines."

Tristan smiled at him. "My cat Lucy loves anchovies," he said. "She was missing, too, you know. She was gone for six months, but we found her in the end. It's really worth staying positive."

Will gave a watery smile. "Thanks," he said. "I'll try."

Melissa, who was sitting on the arm of the couch, suddenly leaned forward. "Is Tiger a playful cat?" she asked shyly. "My rabbit, Rascal, loves her toys." Andi gave her an encouraging smile.

Will nodded. "We've got a rubber mouse on an elastic string that he chases all over the place." He fished under the couch and brought out the mouse, stretching the string until the mouse twanged back and whacked into the couch's leg. "He's got tons of energy and always bugs me to play with him. Oh, and he's got this habit of leaping out of bushes and grabbing at people's ankles. It's really funny."

"We'll start looking for him right away," Tristan said, snapping his notebook shut. "You've looked in the house already, right?"

Will nodded. "But I guess it wouldn't hurt to look again. Especially since you guys are professionals."

The word "professional" made Andi feel very proud. "We'll divide up the inside of the house first," she suggested, with a nod from the others.

The Pet Finders slipped into their practiced house-search routine, with Melissa doing her best to keep up. Andi and Tristan started upstairs, while Natalie and Melissa helped Will downstairs. They opened cupboards, pulled back furniture, looked under beds. They lifted all the drapes in case Tiger was hidden among the folds. They even looked underneath the bathtub, when Tristan found a handle that opened the front panel of the tub.

"Remember when we found a cat behind a bath panel?" he said to Andi as he carefully put the panel back. "It's always worth checking the weirdest places."

But there was no sign of Tiger anywhere.

Andi and Tristan trudged down the stairs. Natalie, Melissa, and Will were waiting anxiously at the bottom.

"No luck." Andi sighed.

"No luck for us either," Will said gloomily. "I'm not surprised. Tiger's really an outdoor cat. He only comes in to play and sleep."

"What happens next?" Melissa asked Natalie.

"We check the yard, ask the neighbors if they've seen anything, borrow a photo of the missing pet, make posters and flyers and put them around the neighborhood, widen our search if we have to, and report the missing pet to the local animal shelter and maybe the police," Natalie rattled off.

"You do all that?" Melissa looked surprised. Natalie nodded. Andi realized it did sound like a lot, though sometimes it felt as if there was never enough they could do to find a missing animal.

She glanced out the window. The rain had eased off, and the sun was shining weakly into the yard. "Next thing we do is check outside," she said. "We'll ask the neighbors if we can check their yards, too."

"We'll find Tiger for you," Melissa said to Will as they all trooped outside. "We'll find him up a tree, I bet. Rascal, my rabbit, seems to be missing all the time. I always totally panic, and then I find her five minutes later."

Finding pets wasn't usually that easy, Andi knew. But Will looked happier at Melissa's confident words, and Andi didn't want to spoil his mood. Crossing her fingers and hoping Melissa was right, she turned her attention to the search.

They picked their way between the shrubs, peered up trees, and poked and prodded the fence for any loose panels. Tristan hunted through the Jacobses' shed, and Natalie and Melissa checked the garage.

Underneath a prickly shrub at the side of the house, Natalie found a clump of brownish-gray fur. "It's a clue!"

Andi took the piece of fluff and held it up to get a better look at it. "I don't think it looks very tabby," she said doubtfully. "Will, what do you think?"

Will looked carefully at it. "Tiger's more golden than that, but he's got gray fur in his undercoat," he said. "You can see it sometimes when you part his fur right down to the skin."

"Can I see?" Melissa took the fur and rubbed it between her fingers. She frowned. "Sorry, guys, but this is rabbit fur," she said, passing it to Tristan.

Andi was impressed. "How do you know?" she asked, taking the fluff from Tristan and rolling it between her fingers, the way she'd seen Melissa do.

"It's much finer than cat fur," Melissa said. "You can hardly feel the fibers when you rub it like this, see? Even really soft cats have thicker fibers in their coats than rabbits do." She suddenly looked upset. "Throw it away, Andi. It's useless."

"Don't worry, Melissa," Tristan said. "That was amazing, the way you read that clue. You're part of the pet-finding team already!"

Melissa shrugged. "But we didn't find Tiger, did we?"

"It's very rare that we find pets just by checking someone's house and yard," Andi reminded everyone.

"But it would have been nice, just this once." Natalie sighed.

"Look at it this way. It could be a good thing that we haven't found Tiger too close to home," Andi said.

Melissa looked baffled. "It is?"

"If you find a cat close to home but not *at* home, it's often because they're injured and can't physically make it those last few yards," Tristan said carefully.

Injured — or worse, Andi felt like adding. She'd once searched for an old hunting dog in Arizona who ended up having found a quiet space under a bush to die. It had been her most upsetting case.

Will looked like he was on the verge of tears.

"Have you tried putting food outside Tiger's catdoor?" Tristan hastily changed the subject. "He might come back, but he may be too scared to come inside. When cats are missing, it's often because they've been traumatized by something. That can make them frightened of everything, even their own home."

"I'll try tonight," Will promised.

"You said Tiger was a bit overweight, right?" Natalie

recalled. "That means he won't be too badly affected by a few days without food, and the layers of fat should keep him warm at night."

"And he's got plenty of water," Melissa pointed out, dipping the tip of her soggy high-top in a nearby puddle.

Natalie hesitated, trying to phrase a delicate question. "Is it possible that Tiger's been adopted by someone else?" She glanced at Tristan. "It happened to Lucy, Tris. We should consider it."

"It's too soon," Andi decided. "Tiger's only been gone a couple of days. If he's still missing a week from now, maybe we should think about that again."

"Tiger wouldn't forget me just like that," Will said uncertainly. "Would he?"

There was an awkward pause. Melissa checked her watch. "Listen, guys," she said, "I have to go feed Rascal. She gets antsy if her food's late. Sorry, Will. I really thought we'd find Tiger for you today." She looked genuinely sad.

"We'll have to miss Dean's pizza," Natalie said.

"We'll come over right after lunch and bring you some," Andi promised. "We can bring Jet over, too, to save you the trip to Tris's house now."

"Perfect," Nat said, as she and Melissa headed off, swinging the closed umbrella between them.

"We should make a poster of Tiger," Andi said. "Do you have a photo we can use, Will?"

"Tiger's a little camera shy," Will said, "but I'll see what I can find. Wait here."

He disappeared for a few minutes. When he came back, he was holding three photographs. "Sorry they aren't that great," he apologized.

One of the pictures showed a glimpse of Tiger's tabby tail as he fled from the camera. Another was a blurry action shot as Tiger jumped up at something which looked like his mouse toy. The third picture was quite small, but it did show all of Tiger.

Andi tucked it inside one of the plastic wallets in Tristan's backpack. "We'll return it as soon as we've made the posters," she promised. "Once we've put them up, we'll question the neighbors and widen our search if we have to. Stay positive, Will. We're only just getting started."

They all turned at the sound of a key in the door. A tall, thin man with the same dark brown eyes as Will came inside and propped his umbrella on the door mat.

"Hi, Dad," Will said. "You're home early."

"The quote didn't take as long as I thought it would," Mr. Jacobs explained, taking off his jacket. "Modern houses aren't nearly as much hassle as the old ones when it comes to air-conditioning. Hi," he said to Andi and Tristan. "Friends of Will, are you?"

Will introduced them and explained about the Pet Finders Club.

"You'd have to be a Saunders with that red hair," Mr. Jacobs said to Tristan, with a friendly smile. "You're the spitting image of your dad. I've worked on air conditioners on a couple of projects for your parents in the past. Anyway, it's great that you're going to help us find Tiger. Have you guys had lunch yet? You're welcome to stay."

"Thanks, Mr. Jacobs, but my brother's expecting us home for pizza now," Tristan explained.

Mr. Jacobs nodded. "Another time, then."

Trying not to shiver too much in the damp air coming from the open front door, Andi told Will, "We'll make posters and flyers as soon as we can. Then we'll be back in touch. And remember — "

"Stay positive," Will said with a determined nod.

After waving good-bye, Andi followed Tristan down the front path. Her sneakers squished, still wet from the walk over. Andi noticed that it was tough to stay positive when there was water seeping between your toes.

Chapter Three

Dean's pizza toppings were creative, to say the least.

"I liked the sausage and jelly combination," Tristan said as they headed to Natalie's house, the dogs trotting at their heels.

"You would," Andi said with a shudder. Even Buddy had turned his head away when she'd offered him her crust, which had a smear of jelly clinging to it.

They walked up the path toward the wide steps and fluted columns of Natalie's house. As always, the front yard looked immaculate. Even the puddles looked perfectly round and shiny.

They entered the house through the garage, since they were so wet. They took off their coats and shoes and put Buddy and Jet in a small room by the backdoor to dry off.

"It's so neat, having this room here," Andi said as she

finished drying off Buddy's feet. Buddy padded over to Jet's roomy basket and collapsed next to Jet with a sigh.

"Only Natalie would have a room dedicated solely to a dog," Tristan agreed. "She told me it used to be the laundry room, but Mrs. Peters got tired of taking the washing up and down the stairs all the time, so they put in a new laundry room upstairs."

"You're keeping the dogs in there, right?" Melissa asked as Andi and Tristan emerged from the dog room. "Rascal would go crazy if she saw them. If she even *smelled* them she'd get scared."

Natalie came down the hall then. Catching Andi's eye, she made a face. She clearly thought Melissa was a little overprotective of her rabbit.

"Hi, guys," Natalie said, taking the foil-wrapped pizza from Andi. "Did you get a picture of Tiger?"

They walked together into the kitchen, where Natalie's mom was talking to Maria, their housekeeper. Maria looked angry.

"Melissa," Mrs. Peters said, looking around, "did you use the bag of radicchio from the crisper drawer for Rascal's lunch?"

Melissa looked worried. "No," she said. "I just took some lettuce."

Maria muttered something in Spanish and vigorously began scrubbing the saucepans in the sink.

Mrs. Peters looked flustered. "Radicchio *is* lettuce. That was for *us* to eat," she said. "It's a bit exotic for a rabbit!"

"Rascal finished her own bag of lettuce, and she was still hungry," Melissa said apologetically. "I'm really sorry."

She slowly unzipped the front of her sweater. A single, telltale leaf of radicchio popped out, followed by a little white nose, and finally the head of a small, pale gray rabbit.

"You must be Rascal," Andi said with delight. "Melissa, she's gorgeous!"

"I know," Melissa said affectionately.

Rascal shook her head, making her ears flap. Wriggling halfway out of Melissa's sweater, she twitched her nose at the housekeeper.

Natalie laughed. "She's trying to tell Maria she's sorry, look!"

Maria's frown disappeared, and she smiled as she came over to stroke Rascal's fur. No one could stay angry with such an adorable little creature.

Melissa cuddled Rascal under her chin. "Let's take you upstairs out of trouble," she said.

All the rabbits Andi knew lived outside in hutches, with wire-mesh runs. An indoor rabbit was a whole new idea. "Does Rascal have a cage?" she asked, as they followed Melissa up the stairs.

"She has a condo back home," Melissa explained.

"What, with a pool and everything?" Tristan joked.

Andi pictured Rascal on a lounge chair with a fruit cocktail in one paw.

Melissa laughed. "No! It's a bunch of wire cages stacked on top of each other. She loves climbing around in it. But when I'm at home, she mostly hops around the house."

Natalie pushed open the door to the game room. "Rascal stays in here ever since she ate my slippers."

"She did *not* eat your slippers!" Melissa insisted.

On the floor in the game room was a cage lined with curly wood shavings and a nest of straw in one corner. Beside the cage was a bowl of water and a dish of food pellets on a plastic mat. Next to them was a litter tray. A couple of long cardboard tubes lay farther away on the rug. It looked like a rabbit vacation resort!

"We've barricaded off all the little spaces Rascal can fit into, so we don't lose her under or behind the furniture," Melissa explained. "She can run around the whole room now, see?" She put Rascal down beside one of the tubes. The little rabbit sniffed at the tube opening, then shot through it and out the other side.

"Impressive!" Andi said as Rascal hopped around and ran through the tube again, this time in the opposite direction.

"That's nothing," Melissa said proudly. "Wait till you see what Nat and I put together for her last night!"

Natalie started looking more enthusiastic and helped Melissa set up a collection of boxes, hoops, and tubes in the middle of the floor. The finishing touch on the obstacle course was a scaled-down seesaw made out of a book and an empty shampoo bottle.

"On the count of three . . . " Melissa said, setting Rascal down at one end of the course.

"Three!" the others shouted.

Rascal zoomed over the book seesaw and shot through the tubes, then hopped over the boxes and through the hoops. Every so often she gave an energetic little sideways kick, for what looked like the sheer fun of it. Andi thought it was one of the cutest things she'd ever seen!

Suddenly, two sets of paws charged up the stairs: one set large, and one set small. The next moment, the door to the game room was shoved open — and Jet and Buddy tumbled in, barking joyfully.

"Rascal!" Melissa gasped, making a dash for her pet. But the little rabbit took one look at the Labrador and fled across the room. Within seconds, she had completely disappeared.

Natalie threw herself on Jet and managed to get a grip on his collar, while Andi grabbed Buddy. They dragged the protesting dogs outside and shut the door, where they started scratching and whining to be let in again.

"Melissa, I'm really sorry," Nat panted. "I checked on Jet before we came upstairs, and I thought I'd shut the door. Where's Rascal?"

"I don't know!" Melissa wailed. "She's disappeared! First Tiger, now Rascal. I must be bad luck or something!"

Natalie kept apologizing, but Melissa was too upset to listen. Andi and Tristan started looking for the little rabbit, upending the cardboard tubes and peering behind the curtains.

"She couldn't have gotten behind the furniture," Natalie said, puzzled. "We blocked everything off. I'm sure we did."

They all stared around the apparently rabbitless room.

Suddenly, Melissa made a dive toward Rascal's cage. "Look!" she said with delight. "She put herself to bed!" Triumphantly, she burrowed her hand into the nest of straw and gently pulled out the little rabbit. Rascal was trembling all the way from her ears to her powderpuff tail, but as Melissa stroked her and murmured soothingly to her, she began to calm down.

"Isn't she smart?" Melissa marveled. "She knew she'd be safe in her cage!"

"We should have looked there first," Andi groaned, staring at the mess they'd made. "Now we'll have to straighten everything up again."

"This is all my fault, Melissa," Natalie said. She looked really upset with herself. "Is Rascal okay?"

"She's fine," said Melissa.

Tristan reached over and stroked Rascal's downy head with one finger. "Poor little thing," he said. "She's still shaking." He looked at Natalie. "I think you should keep Jet downstairs while Rascal's staying here. If Jet got into the game room again, Rascal could get hurt."

Melissa beamed at Tristan. "Thanks," she said. "It's great to have someone understand."

Tristan turned red. "Well, we've already got one lost pet to deal with," he said. "We don't want another one."

Andi and Natalie left the room to take the dogs back downstairs.

Natalie bent down to give Jet a cuddle. "You wouldn't

do that again, would you?" she said, scratching his velvety black ears. "I don't really have to shut you downstairs." She sounded like she was trying to convince herself.

Andi picked up Buddy, who wriggled and tried to lick her face. "Dogs can't help being bigger than rabbits," she said sympathetically to Natalie. "It really would be better to keep Jet downstairs."

"Okay," Natalie said reluctantly. "I'll put him in his dog room. Come on, Jet. Let's go." She stood up and hooked her fingers under Jet's collar to lead him down the stairs. Andi followed her, with Buddy tucked tightly under her arm.

Down in the dog room, Natalie rubbed Jet's tummy, making him squirm with delight. "It seems a little unfair, shutting him in here." She sighed as Andi put Buddy down. "Melissa and Rascal are taking over the whole house."

"It won't be for long," Andi reminded her. "Jet'll be fine. Besides, he loves it in here. Not many dogs have their own rooms."

She went over to tickle Jet's ears. When she turned back to Buddy, the little terrier had vanished.

Andi's first frantic thought was that Buddy had run

upstairs again. But she found him in the kitchen, sitting hopefully at Maria's feet as the housekeeper chopped pieces of meat for a casserole.

"First the radicchio, now the casserole," Andi scolded, picking Buddy up. "If it was up to the animals in this house, Nat's family wouldn't have anything to eat!"

Andi woke up the following day with Buddy enthusiastically licking her face. She squinted up at the unfamiliar ceiling for a moment before she remembered where she was. She and Tristan had stayed up late the previous night to make a poster and a flyer about Tiger. The photo Will had given them wasn't great, but the poster was bright and colorful and was sure to get people's attention.

Pulling back the curtains, Andi saw it was another wet, cold day. Perhaps all those sweaters her mom had packed would come in handy after all. Downstairs, Mr. Saunders was eating toast and looking through the newspaper, while opposite him, Mrs. Saunders was eating cereal and fixing her earrings at the same time.

"Morning!" she called as Tristan and Andi came into the kitchen.

"Pet finding again?" Mr. Saunders studied the stack of posters that Andi had put on the breakfast bar. "Great poster. Shame about the photo. It's a little small."

"I know," Andi said. "I enlarged it as much as I could, but you can hardly see Tiger at all."

"I'll take a poster and a handful of flyers to the office," Mrs. Saunders offered, scooping them up and putting them into her briefcase. "Are you meeting Natalie today?"

"Maybe later. Natalie and her friend Melissa are shopping for party outfits this morning," Andi explained, pouring some juice. Natalie had called the night before to say that she'd changed her mind about her blue beaded dress and needed to find something else. Melissa loved shopping, too, so they were going together. Andi felt a tiny bit relieved that Natalie hadn't asked her to go shopping with them. She knew she wouldn't be able to concentrate on party outfits while Tiger was still missing.

"We'll be back early tonight," Mrs. Saunders said. She winked. "Hopefully I'll be able to save you from one of Dean's culinary wonders."

After breakfast, Andi and Tristan snapped on Buddy's leash and stepped out into the gray morning. Soon, half the trees between Tristan's house and Will's were adorned with posters and the mailboxes stuffed with flyers.

"Hi!" Will came hurrying down the street toward them. He looked tired, like he hadn't slept much. "I've been watching for you. Can I see Tiger's poster?"

Andi showed it to him. "We've put up a lot of them already."

"The picture I gave you turned out really blurry," Will said, looking worried.

"But the rest of the poster's nice and bright," Andi said encouragingly. "People will stop and read them, don't worry. Come on, let's put up a few more of these, and then we'll start talking to your neighbors."

The three of them, plus Buddy, walked down Oakley Avenue, pushing flyers into the remaining mailboxes and attaching posters to trees and telephone poles. As they reached the end of the street, they saw a young woman jogging along the sidewalk toward them.

"Does that lady live on your street?" Andi asked.

Will nodded. "That's Mrs. Olson. She lives in this house here, with the green door."

Mrs. Olson came to a halt as she reached Andi and the others. "Morning, Will!" she said, leaning her hands on her knees to catch her breath. Her long, dark pony-tail swung forward over her shoulder. "What are you up to?"

Will showed her a poster and explained about Tiger. "Have you seen him recently?" he asked hopefully.

Mrs. Olson straightened up. "I'm pretty certain I just saw him last night," she said, to Andi's astonishment.

"You did?" Will asked excitedly. "Where?"

Mrs. Olson frowned. "Behind my house, I think, when I was taking out the trash. But I only caught a glimpse of him in the shadows beside the garage. It might not have been Tiger, but it was definitely a tabby cat."

"That's fantastic news!" Will exclaimed, turning to Andi and Tristan. "Right, guys?"

Andi was excited, too, but she was also experienced enough not to put a great deal of hope on one sighting. "It's a good start," she agreed, smiling at Will. "We'll check out the garage right away."

They thanked Mrs. Olson for her time and walked on around the corner. Will clapped his hands together with delight. "If Mrs. Olson saw Tiger just yesterday," he said, "that means he's still alive!" He was so happy, Andi couldn't bring herself to tell him they could get several false sightings before they found one that really was Tiger.

When they reached the end of Oakley Avenue, Will looked hopefully at Andi and Tristan. "What next?" he asked.

"Let's start asking questions," Andi said.

With so many people away for Spring Break, knocking on the neighbors' doors didn't take long. No one had a golden tabby cat locked in their garage, and there was no point in checking for pawprints in the backyards with all the rain they'd had. After the excitement of Mrs. Olson's news, it was an appropriately gloomy end to the morning.

"I really thought we'd find him, after what Mrs. Olson said," Will said sadly, scuffing the sidewalk with his sneaker. "Mrs. Olson probably didn't see Tiger at all, just some other tabby."

Andi tried to console him. "It's all part of the puzzle. You never know, it could be a vital clue later on." Privately, she suspected that Will's prediction was probably right.

After promising Will they'd call if they heard any more news, Andi and Tristan headed down a long, straight street of grand houses, discreetly shielded by hedges and tall fences. The trees that lined the road were stubbornly refusing to produce buds and looked as cold and bare as they had in January.

Andi was just putting a poster on one of the stately trees when her phone started ringing.

"Andi?" It was Natalie. She sounded breathless. "You have to come over, now!"

"Why? What's happened?"

There was a pause, then Natalie said dramatically, "Andi — Rascal's gone!"

Chapter Four

Andi bundled the string and paper back in her bag, tugged on Buddy's leash, and waved frantically at Tristan, who was putting flyers in mailboxes on the far end of the street. "That was Natalie!" she called. "Rascal's missing!"

"What? When?" Tristan asked anxiously, jogging up to her.

"They couldn't find her after they got back from their shopping trip," Andi explained.

"Poor Melissa. Poor Rascal! Can you imagine being that small and getting lost in a house as big as Nat's?" He paused. "And with a dog as energetic as Jet?"

Andi shook her head. "I don't think Jet would hurt Rascal," she said firmly. "Anyway, after yesterday, I'm sure Nat's being extra careful about keeping him in the dog room."

They reached Natalie's street a little while later and ran up the path that led to her front door. The door opened just a crack before Andi had even touched the doorbell.

"I can't open it any wider, in case Rascal's in here somewhere and gets out," Natalie explained through the narrow gap. She opened the door just enough for Andi and Tristan to squeeze inside before shutting the door quickly behind them. "Melissa's really upset, because she thinks it's all her fault."

"What happened?" Andi asked, putting Buddy in the dog room with Jet.

"Melissa was playing with Rascal in the game room when her mom called from Europe," Natalie reported. "Melissa went downstairs to take the call. Maria was vacuuming the landing."

"And Melissa left the door open?" Tristan guessed. He sounded surprised. "I thought she'd be extra careful after yesterday!"

Natalie shook her head. "No, she closed the door, but the nearest outlet for the vacuum plug was in the game room, and she couldn't shut the door on the cord, so there was a tiny gap. I guess that was enough for Rascal to escape, because when Melissa got back from talking on the phone, Rascal was gone."

Tristan opened his mouth, but Natalie held up her hand. "If you're going to ask about Jet, don't bother," she said. "He was shut up in the dog room the whole time."

There was a mournful bark from inside the dog room when Jet heard his name.

"Is that Andi and Tristan?" Melissa called from the top of the stairs. She came halfway down and stopped. Her eyes were red and swollen, and she looked utterly miserable.

"Pet Finders to the rescue!" Andi declared. "Where should we start looking?"

"We looked around the game room already," Natalie said, as they all trooped upstairs to join Melissa. "But we could check again."

"There are two options," Andi said briskly, pushing open the game room door. "One, Rascal is still somewhere in the game room. Two, she got out through the gap in the door. The spaces behind the furniture in here are all blocked off, right?" Natalie and Melissa nodded. "So, when we finish checking in here, we should block off all the other small spaces around the house as soon as we've checked them out," Andi said. "Lock cupboards after we've searched them, stuff like that. Just in case Rascal doubles back and hides where we already looked."

Natalie went to the corner of the game room and pulled out a box of old vinyl records in square cardboard jackets. "We could use these to block any gaps," she suggested. "Rascal couldn't jump over them."

After a thorough hunt around the game room to confirm that the little rabbit wasn't hiding behind the drapes or inside a cardboard tube, they began to move through the upper story of the house. Andi got down on her hands and knees to peer underneath the heavy drapes next to the windows on the landing. Beside her, Tristan checked behind a bureau, then blocked off the narrow gaps between the bureau and the wall and the bottom of the bureau and the rug. They all gathered to check Natalie's bedroom next, although Nat acted a little strange when Andi wanted to check her closet.

"The door's been locked since before Rascal disappeared," she insisted. "There's no point wasting time in there."

They checked all the other rooms' closets and drawers, shutting every door firmly behind them. Then they repeated their search downstairs. At last, they ran out of places to look. Feeling defeated, they slumped down on the couch in the sunroom.

"What if Rascal has gotten outside?" Melissa fretted. She looked through the window at the Peterses' spacious backyard. "She doesn't know how to survive outdoors."

Andi squeezed her arm comfortingly. "Don't worry about that yet," she said. "Rascal hasn't been missing long."

"We should put food in all the rooms, in case we can tempt her out of hiding," Natalie suggested.

Melissa pulled open the refrigerator and took out a bag of carrot tops. "Maria saved these from dinner last night," she said. "They're Rascal's favorite."

They each took a handful of carrot tops, then walked around the house, placing the food in the middle of each room. When they reached Mr. Peters's study, they found Maria vacuuming underneath the desk. Natalie put down the carrot top beside the door and tapped her on the shoulder. "Maria?"

Maria flipped the switch on the vacuum cleaner and the room fell silent. "You are still looking for the little rabbit?" she asked sadly. "I am so sorry about what happened."

"It was really bad luck," Natalie agreed. "Could you stop cleaning for about a half hour? Rascal is more likely to come out of hiding if the house is quiet."

"Sure. I can go speak with John about the flowers for

the party instead," said Maria. John was the Peterses' gardener.

"Let's wait in the kitchen," Andi said as Maria went into the yard. "We can check the carrot tops after we've given Rascal a chance to smell them and come out from wherever she's hiding."

They tiptoed back to the kitchen, shutting the door as quietly as they could. Tristan headed straight for the refrigerator and made sandwiches for everyone. Then they sat and watched the kitchen clock.

"Have you ever found a rabbit before?" Melissa asked hopefully.

"We found Smokey," Tristan said at once. He had one of those memories that never forgot a thing. "Remember when all the animals in the pet store were missing?" he reminded Andi and Natalie. "Smokey was the gray lop-eared rabbit that turned up in a construction worker's jacket."

Melissa's eyes widened. "A whole pet store of animals was missing? And you found them all?"

"Technically, the construction worker found Smokey," Andi admitted. They didn't have any direct experience in finding rabbits, she realized a little unhappily. She tried to remember if they'd had any similar cases to

Rascal. They had had a lot of trouble tracking down the school hamster one time. The problem with small animals, like guinea pigs, hamsters, and rabbits, was that they got scared really easily and didn't come when you called their names. They were so little, too, and moved really fast. Not to mention that there was an added danger from predators like foxes.

Andi sighed. None of these thoughts was very encouraging.

When they had finished their sandwiches, it was only twenty minutes since they'd put the carrot tops down, so, even though it was unlikely that Rascal had gotten outside, they made a sweep of the backyard. In addition to the generous length of lawn, there were lots of large shrubs and trees to check around, but there was no sign of Rascal anywhere.

When they came back inside, twenty more minutes had passed.

"Rascal has to have found the carrot tops by now, right?" Melissa said. Andi winced to see how hopeful she was — tempting a scared rabbit out of hiding with a few vegetable scraps was a bit of a long shot.

The first room they checked was the downstairs bathroom.

"I don't believe it!" Andi whispered.

The carrot top was gone.

"Rascal!" Melissa cried in delight, then clapped her hands over her mouth as Natalie and Tristan waved their hands and made shushing noises at her. They couldn't scare Rascal away now!

The hunt was on. Carrot tops were missing from the dining room, the den, and the living room. They raced upstairs. Sure enough, carrot tops were missing from the game room and Natalie's bedroom as well.

"How can Rascal be moving around the house so fast?" Tristan said in exasperation as they stared at the empty floor.

"Natalie? Melissa?" Mrs. Peters put her head around the bedroom door. "Can you explain what all these carrot tops are doing littered around the house?" She had two carrot tops in her hands, holding them away from her as if they were contaminated. "There's no sign of Maria, so I've been everywhere, cleaning them up. Can you please just feed Rascal in the kitchen in the future? We're trying to make the house spotless for the party on Friday. I've had to cancel all my client meetings this week because there's so much work to do. And carrots stain the rugs!"

"You cleaned up all the carrots?" Natalie asked in dismay. "But we're trying to find Rascal, Mom! She's never going to come out if there's no food for her."

Mrs. Peters blinked. "Rascal's disappeared? Oh, Melissa, I'm sorry. I had no idea! Why don't we go into the kitchen and find some celery instead? Rabbits love celery, don't they?"

"And it won't stain the rug," Tristan murmured to Andi as they followed Mrs. Peters to the kitchen. Melissa had gotten very quiet and looked sad. It really did feel like they were back to square one.

But the Pet Finders didn't give up that easily. They started over, this time putting chunks of celery all around the house. They decided to wait in Natalie's bedroom for Rascal to come out of hiding; it was the room closest to the game room, so it made sense that Rascal could have gone there first.

"We really should check your closet, Nat," said Andi.

"No, wait — " Nat began, but Andi ignored her and reached for the door handle. She turned it and swung open the door.

"Help!" she spluttered, as sweaters, T-shirts, and pants tumbled out of the closet and fell on her head like a tidal wave of fabric.

Natalie looked embarrassed. "I told you not to bother,"

she said. "I can hardly get inside there myself, let alone Rascal. Hey!" She pounced on a pair of shoes that had fallen on top of the heap. "I've been looking for these for ages!"

"Why do you have so many clothes, Nat?" Tristan asked, curious.

"Oh, you know, some of us like to vary our outfits." Natalie stared pointedly at Tristan's red skateboarder T-shirt, which he'd worn practically every day that week.

After waiting a little longer, the Pet Finders made another sweep of the house. The chunks of celery were exactly where they had left them. Either Rascal was too scared to come out of hiding — or she wasn't around to smell them.

"We've done as much as we can today," Andi sighed. "It's up to Rascal now. If she wants to come out, she'll come out."

"No Tiger, and now no Rascal," Melissa said sadly. "We're not doing much pet finding today, are we?"

There was nothing Andi could say to disagree.

Andi was deep in a dream about catching Rascal. Every time she got close, the little rabbit gave one of her cute sideways kicks and leaped out of reach.

Suddenly, the chase was interrupted by the chirp of a cell phone. Sitting bolt upright, Andi snatched it up. "Nat?" she said, rubbing her eyes. "Did you catch her?"

"Hello?" said a soft, elderly-sounding voice. "Is this the Pet Finders Club?"

"Sorry, I thought you were someone else," Andi said hurriedly. "Can I help you?"

"I hope so," said the voice. "My name is Mrs. Shelley Greenstreet. My neighbor saw your flyer about a missing cat?"

"Yes, that's a case we're working on now." Andi felt a tingle of hope. "Have you seen Tiger?"

"I'm afraid not," Mrs. Greenstreet said apologetically. "But there may be some kind of connection. I've lost my cat as well, you see, and I wondered if you might be able to find her for me."

"We'll do our best," Andi promised. Another case! Spring Break was certainly a busy time for lost pets. She reached for a pencil and carefully wrote down Mrs. Greenstreet's address. "We'll be over in about an hour," she promised.

As soon as Mrs. Greenstreet hung up, Andi ran into the bathroom and jumped into the shower. Then she went to wake up Tristan.

He sat up blearily. "Where's the fire?"

"No fire," Andi said. "But we've got another missing cat. Come on, get up!"

While Tristan took a shower, Andi called Natalie.

"There's still no sign of Rascal," Natalie reported, sounding tired. "Melissa and I were up until midnight looking for her."

"Was the celery still there?" Andi asked.

"Yup, every last piece." Natalie yawned. "We put a bowl of rabbit food in the sunroom today, instead, in case Rascal likes that better."

Andi told her about the call from Mrs. Greenstreet. "Why don't you bring Melissa?" she suggested. "It might take her mind off Rascal."

Natalie promised they'd be ready in half an hour. Andi checked a map to find Mrs. Greenstreet's house. "It's not too far from Will's place." She showed Tristan. "We could make some house calls about Tiger afterward."

Tristan looked down at the piece of paper where Andi had written Mrs. Greenstreet's address. "Hey, I recognize this," he said. "Christine delivers cat food to this house on the first Thursday of every month. I don't think Mrs. Greenstreet has ever come into the store when I've been there, though. I'll call Christine on the way and tell her we're heading over there. She'll be really sad if Mrs. Greenstreet has lost her cat."

Andi put Buddy on his leash while Tristan took his skateboard from the closet under the stairs, and they set out. Andi ended up jogging most of the way, partly to give Buddy a good run and partly to keep up with Tristan, who was trying high-speed maneuvers up and down the curb. They reached the Peterses' house double quick, and luckily Natalie and Melissa were already waiting for them. Natalie had Jet on his leash, and the Labrador bounced around like a fish on a line when he saw Buddy running along the sidewalk.

"Thanks for coming with us," Andi said to Melissa. "You were great when we interviewed Will about Tiger."

Melissa looked pleased and managed a faint smile.

It was a twenty-minute walk to Mrs. Greenstreet's house — a neat, white one-story with a rocker on the porch. They tied the dogs to the porch rail and rang the bell. The door was opened by a small, plump woman with curly, iron-gray hair, wearing a blue flowered blouse and comfortable-looking leather slippers.

"How kind of you to come," Mrs. Greenstreet said after introductions had been made. She stood aside to let them in. "I'm getting very worried about Whiskers. She's been missing for several days now."

They walked into a cozy living room with a pink rug on the floor. There was a cool digital radio on the mantelpiece, and a tray of cookies stood waiting on the coffee table.

Mrs. Greenstreet put her hand out and eased herself into a well-worn blue chair beside the fire. As Andi and the others sat down on the long blue couch opposite her, she noticed Mrs. Greenstreet was absently stroking a pink, fleecy blanket folded over the arm of the chair.

"Whiskers adopted me about three months ago," she began, after Tristan invited her to tell them all about her pet. "I never really cared for cats, but then Whiskers came into my life and now I can't imagine what I'd do without her. We spend hours in here, listening to the radio. She's terribly lazy and spends most of her time curled up on her blanket, but that just makes her the sweetest, gentlest companion."

"What are her regular habits?" Melissa asked.

Mrs. Greenstreet thought for a moment. "Well, I suppose she does the usual sorts of cat things. She always comes in for her midday meal, and then we spend the afternoon together. She's never around at night, so I guess that's when she goes off catching mice. I don't like to interfere with her routine — if she wants to go out, then out she goes!"

"Do you have a photograph of Whiskers?" said Natalie.

Mrs. Greenstreet gave a gentle smile. "I'm sorry, I don't have any photographs at all."

Glancing around the cozy little room, Andi realized with a shock there wasn't a single photograph to be seen. "What does Whiskers look like?" she prompted.

"Well, she has the softest fur. And such long whiskers! They tickle me even when she's sitting some distance away. Oh, and her ears are very round and neat."

Andi frowned. It was an unusual description. "What color is she?" she ventured. "Calico? Black and white? Tabby?"

"Brown tabby, I think," Mrs. Greenstreet said. "Do have a cookie. I made them yesterday."

"When you say 'brown tabby'," Andi said, "do you mean — "

The kettle started whistling in the kitchen. Mrs. Greenstreet stood up. "I'll be back in a moment. I expect you'd prefer a glass of juice to tea, wouldn't you?"

"Yes, please," said Natalie and Tristan.

Andi followed her into the small, tidy kitchen. "Can I help?" she offered. Glancing around the room, she noticed two bowls on the floor — one half full of water, while the other had a few crumbs of cat food left at the bottom. There was also a cat bed underneath the window.

Mrs. Greenstreet had lined up four glasses on the countertop and was pouring juice. There was something odd about the way she held the tips of her fingers just inside the rims of the glasses. It was as if Mrs. Greenstreet could only judge how far she had filled each one by feeling the juice touch her finger.

Suddenly, Andi understood. Mrs. Greenstreet was blind!

Andi rushed forward. "Can I help you with anything?" she asked. "It must be difficult for you, not being able to see. I mean . . . " She trailed off awkwardly.

Mrs. Greenstreet stretched out her hand, found Andi's arm, and patted it. "I can manage just fine," she said with a warm smile.

She carried the tray of glasses back into the living room, and Andi watched her place it squarely on the coffee table as if she could see perfectly.

Then something else struck Andi. No wonder Mrs. Greenstreet had given such a curious description of her pet — she had never set eyes on her own cat! This was going to be one of their most unusual cases ever!

Chapter Five

"I never realized!" Tristan exclaimed in astonishment as they walked down Main Street. "She didn't act blind."

"I know," Andi agreed. They were going to pick up a cake from the Banana Beach Café. "She hides it so well, doesn't she?"

"How could a blind person describe her pet?" Natalie asked.

"Didn't you notice?" Andi said. "She described the way Whiskers *felt*. She described that perfectly."

"But how does she know Whiskers is a tabby?" Natalie persisted.

"Someone must have told her," Andi guessed.

"She didn't sound very interested in what Whiskers looked like," Tristan said.

"I don't think Mrs. Greenstreet *is* interested in what

Whiskers looks like," Andi said. "Just what she *feels* like. Being blind, that makes total sense."

The cheerful awning and bright rainbow-colored umbrellas outside the Banana Beach Café were a welcome relief from the heavy, colorless day. Dark clouds overhead rumbled ominously as Natalie pushed open the door.

"Bananas!" A blue-and-green parrot clicked its beak at them from a perch beside the bar. "More bananas!"

Melissa stared around, looking stunned. There were straw umbrellas over each table, and bunches of bananas hung on hooks above the bar. Pictures of white, sandy beaches and aqua-blue water were placed around the walls, and reggae music pulsed softly from the stereo. "I feel like I'm on vacation!" she laughed.

Andi laughed with her. "I know what you mean," she said, reaching up to stroke the parrot's glossy blue-and-green feathers. "This is Long John Silver," she told Melissa.

Buddy jumped up happily to greet the parrot. Long John Silver studied him with a wary eye, then clicked his beak and sidled as far away from the excitable terrier as he could.

Tristan looked longingly at the pecan-and-banana muffins on display in the glass cabinet.

"No snacks," Natalie said firmly. "We're here to pick up the cake Mom ordered for the party, and that's it. We have three pets to find, remember?"

Tristan sighed theatrically and sank down at one of the café tables.

"Come to pick up the cake?" Jango Pearce, a tall Jamaican man with grizzled hair, came out of the back room and smiled at them. "Maggie's just putting the finishing touches on it now."

"Not as easy as it sounds when your son is trying to eat all the icing," Maggie Pearce declared, coming out of the kitchen with a large box. "Really, Fisher, how old are you?"

Fisher Pearce, the veterinarian who ran the local ASPCA center, followed his mother through the beaded curtain, licking his fingers. "Never too old for the icing on your cakes, Mom," he said.

"Hi, Fisher!" Andi called.

Fisher grinned. "Hey! How's the pet-finding business?"

Natalie introduced Melissa, and they explained about Rascal, and Tiger, and Whiskers. Fisher whistled through his teeth. "Very busy, then," he commented.

"We're pretty sure Rascal's hiding somewhere in my house," Natalie told him. "What do you think?"

"That would fit with domestic rabbit behavior," he

agreed. "They like small spaces because they make them feel safe from larger predators. Once she knows there aren't any foxes running around your house, I'm sure she'll come out." He smiled at Melissa, who tried to smile back.

"And what about these cats?" Fisher prompted. "How's the search going for them?"

"There was a possible sighting of Tiger a couple of nights ago, but nothing since," Andi said. "We haven't started looking for Whiskers yet — we've only just spoken with his owner."

Fisher looked thoughtful. "Two cats missing within a few days? I don't like the sound of that. You could be dealing with catnappers."

"What, someone stealing cats?" said Natalie, sounding surprised.

Fisher nodded.

"But Tiger and Whiskers aren't pedigreed cats," Tristan pointed out. "Why would anyone want to steal them?"

"Well, you can make money from cats without breeding them," Fisher said. "The thief might ask for a ransom."

Melissa and Natalie gasped and Andi gulped. "They'd have to be real nasty for that."

"Thieves *are* nasty," Fisher said. "You should know that by now. Promise me you won't go looking for trouble?"

"Don't worry," Andi reassured him.

"Good," Fisher said, looking relieved. "So, what's the plan? Running three cases at the same time must be pretty tough."

"We've left food out for Rascal at home, so we can look for Tiger and Whiskers this morning," said Natalie. She turned to the others. "Why don't we split into pairs, one pair to look for Tiger and the other to look for Whiskers?"

As they nodded, Fisher suggested, "You could try asking if anyone else has lost a cat recently. Maybe you could put up a notice about it in the convenience store. I'm sure Rocky would let you."

"That's a good idea. Thanks, Fisher," Andi said, getting to her feet. "We'd better get going. Oh!"

A loud clap of thunder made them all jump. Jet whined and retreated underneath Nat's chair, while Buddy jumped up and scraped at Andi's leg with his paw. Outside, the sky looked almost black, and rain began pelting against the café windows.

"Did anyone bring an umbrella?" asked Natalie.

The others shook their heads.

"I hope Rascal isn't outside!" Melissa said anxiously.

Not just Rascal — Andi's stomach flipped over as she thought about the two lost cats, bedraggled and miserable in the rain.

"Looks like we're stuck here for a while," Tristan said. "Banana-and-pecan muffins for everyone?"

After half an hour, the rain showed no signs of letting up, so Maggie lent them a large, striped umbrella. At least they could keep the cake dry on the way back to the Peterses' house, although the umbrella was only big enough to shelter two people. Andi and Tristan volunteered to get wet, so Natalie and Melissa shared the umbrella and carried the cake gingerly between them.

"You're soaked!" Mrs. Peters declared when she saw Andi and Tristan dripping on the porch. Apart from their sneakers and socks, Natalie and Melissa were perfectly dry. "Come in and take off those wet things," she said. "Natalie will let you borrow some clothes."

"I don't need anything," Tristan said hurriedly.

"I'm sure Nat's got some non-girl stuff," Andi said. She shooed Buddy into the dog room and gave him a brisk rub with a towel. "Right, Nat?"

After a bit of grumbling, Tristan chose a crimson sweatshirt with a funky surf logo and some old jeans that were a little short in the leg. Andi opted for a pair of green, silky cargo pants, a lilac T-shirt, and a blue cashmere sweater. While they were getting changed, Melissa rushed around the house to see if Rascal had eaten any of the food they'd set out, but everything was just as they had left it that morning. She was getting better at coping with the disappointment, but she still looked sad.

"We can't look for Tiger and Whiskers in this weather, either," Tristan said gloomily, as they stood around Natalie's kitchen munching on cheese-and-tomato sandwiches. The rain was rushing along the gutters and pouring down the windows in small waterfalls. "They'll be even harder to find if they've found somewhere out of the rain to hide."

"Why don't we call Will and Mrs. Greenstreet and tell them that we'll come over tomorrow?" Natalie suggested. "We can still split into pairs so we cover both cases at the same time."

Andi took out her cell phone and made the calls. Mrs. Greenstreet was out, so she left a message on her voice mail. Will Jacobs picked up the phone on the second ring.

"Any news?" he said eagerly.

Andi felt a pang of guilt. "Not exactly," she said. "The

weather's a problem. If it's dry tomorrow, Tristan and I will start doing the door-to-door inquiries. We need to widen our search." Andi knew she had to phrase her next piece of news carefully. "Listen, Will, we have another missing cat case," she said. "We're splitting up tomorrow to run two searches at the same time. I don't want to worry you, but there are signs that we could be dealing with a catnapper."

"You mean, someone might have *stolen* Tiger?"

"Maybe."

There was a pause. "Well, I guess we shouldn't stop looking for him, just in case," Will said bravely. "See you tomorrow."

As Andi hung up, Mrs. Peters came into the kitchen. She was carrying an armful of snowy-white linen napkins. "Are you busy?" she asked.

They shook their heads. "Would you help me by folding these?" she said, placing the napkins on the table.

"The party's still two days away, Mom," Natalie pointed out.

"I know." Mrs. Peters pushed a hand through her shiny blond hair. "But it's all about preparation, and I have a lot to do. Now, where are my raincoat and boots? I'm trying to decide whether to use the greenery that grows by the back fence to decorate the stairs, but if it doesn't work, I have to make a decision today so the florist will be able to supply what I need in time. Oh, this weather!"

Andi stared at the pile of napkins when Mrs. Peters had gone. "There must be a hundred of these," she said. Just how many people did the Peterses know?

"One hundred and four," Natalie replied, as her mom came back through the kitchen with a long, hooded raincoat and boots and disappeared into the sunroom, where there was a door to the backyard. "I told you it was going to be a big party."

"Big?" Tristan echoed, reaching for an apple from the fruit bowl. "This is going to be like the Oscars!" He thrust the apple away in disgust. "Someone's taken a bite out of this already!"

He showed them a neat row of tooth marks in the side of the apple.

Melissa jumped up. "They look like *rabbit* tooth marks!" she said, grabbing the apple and gazing at the neat little grooves in the russet-colored skin. "Shut the door, Natalie. Rascal must be in here!"

Everyone leaped out of their seats and stared around the kitchen. Natalie shut the doors to the hall and the sunroom while Melissa started pulling open the cupboards. Andi and Tristan helped her, taking out cans

and boxes and putting them on the floor so they could see all the way to the back. Andi thought she spotted some rabbit droppings on the bottom shelf, but they turned out to be raisins.

When they'd emptied the entire food cupboard, Melissa sat back and stared in frustration at the boxes of food. "Those tooth marks must be Rascal's. She's *definitely* in here. But where?"

The sunroom door opened. Mrs. Peters stood in the doorway, looking annoyed and so wet she was leaving a puddle on the floor. "How many times," she said with a sigh, "have I asked you to eat your breakfast in the kitchen, Natalie? You've made the most terrible mess in the sunroom. The floor in there is bad enough already with all this rain and mud, and now there's cereal everywhere."

Natalie turned red. "Sorry, Mom," she said. She paused, then swung around to Melissa. "Did we have cereal this morning?"

Melissa frowned. "We both had toast, didn't we?"

Something clicked in Andi's brain. If the mess wasn't cereal, it must be —

"Rabbit food!" Melissa cried. "I forgot to check the bowl of food I left in the sunroom!"

They rushed out of the kitchen, and Andi and Tristan

seized one end of the long wicker couch while Melissa and Natalie took the other. They pulled the couch out from the wall. Behind it, Rascal's bowl of food was tipped on its side, scattering oat flakes across the floor. It looked a bit like granola, which explained Mrs. Peters's mistake.

"Rascal must have started out with the fruit bowl in the kitchen — " Natalie began.

"And then come in here!" Melissa continued, her eyes shining.

Andi felt a damp draft coming from behind her. The door leading out to the backyard was wide open.

"Mom, when did you open this door?" Natalie called to her mother.

"It's been open all morning," Mrs. Peters said, adjusting her coat and preparing to step outside again.

Andi stared at the others in horror. This could spell disaster!

"Mom!" Natalie said, making a visible effort to stay calm. "Remember I told you that Rascal was missing? You shouldn't have left the door open! She might have gotten out into the yard!"

"I'm very sorry about Rascal, but I have to get everything ready for the party, Natalie," Mrs. Peters said gently. "The greenery won't fix itself."

Melissa's eyes flooded with tears. "But Rascal doesn't know about being outdoors!" she said. "She'll be so scared!"

"There's no point worrying about that now," Andi said before Melissa broke down completely. "We'll just have to look outside again. Come on."

They fitted themselves with rain gear and headed outside. The rain had lightened up, but it was still falling softly. Andi surveyed the yard. They'd made a brief sweep the day before, but now that it looked like Rascal really *had* gotten outside, it was time to get serious. Where to start? The shrubs suddenly looked very big and full of potential hiding places for rabbits.

"Let's use the dogs," Natalie suggested.

"No! If they find Rascal, they'll scare her!" Melissa wailed.

"We'll put them on leashes," Andi promised. "It's a great idea — we can use their noses to sniff out Rascal's trail."

Jet was overjoyed to be let out of the dog room, and it took Natalie several minutes to calm him enough to put on his extendable leash. Buddy's leash didn't extend, but it was long enough to allow him to sniff around the bushes. Holding tightly to the leashes, Andi and Natalie led the dogs outside, with Tristan and Melissa following close behind. Melissa carried a tub of dry rabbit food, which she shook as she called Rascal's name.

"We should concentrate on this end of the yard, closest to the house first," Andi decided. "If Rascal's never been outside before, I think she'd head for the nearest hiding place."

They started walking slowly across the lawn. Jet ran in circles, his nose to the ground and his tail wagging like crazy, while Buddy pulled Andi toward a bed of shrubs. Jet yelped and hurtled after them. Soon, both dogs were sniffing excitedly at the largest bush.

The thicket of glossy green leaves was too dense to see underneath just by lifting the outer branches. Andi stared at the muddy soil at the base of the shrubs. There was just enough space for someone to wriggle through on their stomach.

"Time for one of us to get dirty," she said. "Tris?"

"Why me?" Tristan protested.

"You're always a little grubby," Nat said. "Anyway, you said you didn't like the clothes I lent you, so what's the big deal?"

Tristan plucked at the crimson sweatshirt underneath his coat. "It's growing on me," he said.

"Go on," Andi pleaded. "Nat and I are holding the dogs, so we can't do it — and Melissa's a guest Pet

Finder, so we can't make her do the muddy stuff. Pretend you're doing army training or something."

"I may be gone a long time." Tristan sighed, hitching up the legs of his jeans and hunkering down. "If I don't come out, tell Dean he can have my stereo — "

"Get going!" Andi said, giving him a nudge. Tristan lowered himself onto his belly and inched under the leaves. Soon, all they could see were his feet. Andi held her breath, imagining the little rabbit cowering and frightened in the damp and the shadows.

"We're coming!" she called softly. "Don't worry, little one. You'll soon be safe!"

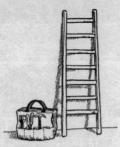

Chapter Six

"Can you see anything?" Melissa called.

"Euw!" Tristan wriggled backward out of the shrubbery in a rush, his face screwed up and mud all over him. "There's a dead bird under there. That must be what the dogs could smell. Sorry, guys."

Melissa's shoulders slumped, and Natalie went over to comfort her. Andi hunkered down and tried to look underneath the leaves. "How did it die?"

"I didn't ask it." Tristan looked queasy. "I think something had been eating it."

"What, like a fox?" Andi said without thinking.

With a horrified cry, Melissa wrenched away from Natalie and ran back to the house in tears. Andi, Tristan, and Natalie looked at each other.

"If there's a fox around," Natalie said grimly, "then Rascal doesn't stand a chance."

She tugged on Jet's leash and followed Melissa into the house. Andi and Tristan continued combing the yard, just in case. The rain steadily grew worse, and the daylight began to fade. They decided to abandon the search and make a fresh start the following day.

Melissa and Natalie were sitting at the kitchen table, slowly folding napkins. Melissa's eyes were red and puffy.

"The good news is that there's no sign of a rabbit in the yard, dead or alive," Andi announced, trying to sound cheerful for Melissa's sake.

Melissa sniffed, and a tear rolled down her nose and plopped onto one of the napkins. "I miss her so much," she whispered. "She's so little and helpless."

Andi and Tristan's clothes had been put through the dryer and were folded neatly on the kitchen table, waiting for them. "We'd better get changed," Tristan said to Andi, "and then we have to go. Dean's making cheese straws shaped like fours and zeros for the party, and we'd better check to be sure he's not including any weird ingredients."

"Fours and zeros?" Natalie echoed.

Tristan beamed. "To spell out your stepdad's age," he said. "Great, huh? Listen, try and stay positive, Melissa. Remember what Fisher said about rabbits liking small spaces? Why would Rascal choose a big wet space like the backyard when there are plenty of small dry ones inside the house?"

"I'll call you tomorrow, Nat," Andi said. "We've still got two cats to find, remember?"

"A good day of pet finding might keep us all from sulking about Rascal," Tristan added. "Imagine if we find both Tiger and Whiskers tomorrow! Stranger things have happened."

Andi felt a little more hopeful. As Tristan was fond of saying, tomorrow was another day.

To Andi's relief, the next day was brighter, and it had stopped raining at last. Flinging back the quilt, she reached for her cell phone to call Natalie. The phone rang while she was scrolling down for Nat's number.

"Andi?" It was Natalie. "You have to get over here, fast!"

"Have you found Rascal?"

"Not yet, no," Natalie said. "But we went out to the yard early this morning to see if we missed any clues yesterday, and we saw this guy in the yard next door."

Andi was hopping around the room trying to pull on her clothes with one hand. "So why do I have to come over right now?"

Natalie lowered her voice. "I know for a fact that Mr. and Mrs. Holland are away for Spring Break, so what's a stranger doing in their yard?"

"It does sound like the kind of thing Fisher told us to look out for," Andi agreed. "But we're looking for a cat-napper, not a rabbitnapper, aren't we?"

"That's just it!" Natalie sounded triumphant. "Mr. and Mrs. Holland have *two* cats. Valuable ones, too. I think they're Burmese or something."

Andi's heart started thudding. This could be a really important lead. "Don't try to talk to him!" she warned Natalie, hurrying down the hall to bang on Tristan's bedroom door with her free hand. "We'll be over as soon as we can!"

News that they could be hot on the trail of the cat-napper made Tristan leap out of bed and pull on his clothes in record time. "We'll ask Mom for a ride," Tristan said as they raced downstairs.

Andi jumped the last two steps. Just as she landed, her cell phone started ringing again. This time it was Will Jacobs.

"Dad had to go out, but he said he'd be back later this morning," Will said. "Mom's home and ready to help with the neighborhood search. What time are you coming over?"

"How about eleven o'clock?" Andi suggested. "We've got to check out some guy that's been seen near Natalie's house, but we'll come by right after."

"What guy?" Will demanded. "Do you think he's the catnapper? Because I'll come check him out, too! At Natalie's house, you said? Where's that?"

"Don't get too excited, Will," Andi warned him, but she did give him Natalie's address. "We'll need to be really careful if we do suspect him of being a thief."

"I'll bike over right away," Will said, then hung up.

"The Pet Finders Club has never had so many members!" Tristan remarked.

Mrs. Saunders looked up as they entered the kitchen. "There are waffles on the table if you want them," she said.

"Thanks, Mom," Tristan said. "Could you give us a ride to Natalie's house?"

"If you're ready to go in exactly ten minutes," Mrs. Saunders warned.

Andi and Tristan raced through their breakfast, fed the animals, brushed their teeth, and combed their hair faster than ever. Luckily, Mrs. Saunders was still waiting for them, jingling her car keys.

"Natalie and Melissa saw someone acting weird in the neighbors' backyard," Tristan explained as his mom steered the car out of the driveway. "We're looking for a catnapper, and it sounds like we could have a suspect."

"What? Don't you dare approach him on your own, do you hear me?" said Mrs. Saunders. "I don't have time to come in right now, but I'll call Mr. Peters when I get to the office and ask him to go with you."

Tristan rolled his eyes. "What is it with adults that they think we'll run headfirst into trouble all the time?"

"We know you too well," Mrs. Saunders replied. She pulled into Natalie's driveway.

"Thanks for the ride, Mrs. Saunders," Andi said as Buddy scrambled to get out of the car first. "We promise not to get into trouble, okay?"

Melissa opened the front door, looking even sadder and paler than the day before. Andi realized she'd been so excited about the new catnapper clue that she'd forgotten how bad Melissa must be feeling. Rascal had been missing for two nights now.

"Did you see any sign of Rascal in the yard?" she asked.

Melissa wiped her eyes. "We found some tufts of fur, but they were the wrong color. Natalie thought maybe they belonged to the Hollands' cats."

Andi wondered uneasily if two cats could hurt a small rabbit. She knew that the answer was yes. Especially if the Hollands' cats were Burmese, as Natalie said. They had a reputation for being ferocious hunters, often bringing down birds as big as themselves.

"We found rabbit pawprints, too," Melissa continued as they walked into the kitchen. "But they could have been made by wild rabbits."

Andi put her hand on Melissa's arm. "I lost Buddy when I first moved to Orchard Park," she said, "and Tristan lost Lucy for almost six months. Nat even lost Jet one time. I know it's hard to stay positive, especially when we're following up a clue that doesn't have anything to do with Rascal. But I promise we all know how you're feeling right now."

"Thanks," Melissa said, trying to smile.

The sunroom door clattered open, and Natalie came rushing into the kitchen. "The guy's still there!" she announced. "He has a ladder propped against the side of the Hollands' house! Suspicious or *what*?"

"Is your stepdad around, Nat?" Andi asked.

"I already asked him to come with us if we go next door," Natalie said promptly, guessing what Andi was going to say next. "He's ready to go as soon as we say."

Andi squared her shoulders. If this guy was the catnapper, they had to catch him quickly. "Let's do it," she said.

Mr. Peters was a tall, easygoing man with a deep tan and eyes that crinkled in a friendly way when he smiled. He worked from a home office three days a week, so he was often around when Andi went over to Natalie's house. Today, he appeared from his study when Natalie knocked on the door, and together they walked down the street to the Hollands' house. They left both dogs at Natalie's house, in case they barked and gave the thief a warning that someone was coming.

The Hollands had an old house built in a beautiful, colonial style, with a colonnaded front and a neatly mowed yard. The driveway was empty, which wasn't surprising if they'd gone away for Spring Break.

There was a squeal of bicycle brakes, and Will Jacobs hurtled up. "I came as quickly as I could!" he said, breathing hard. "Did you confront him yet?"

Natalie introduced Will to her stepdad. "Confrontation won't be necessary," Mr. Peters said. "This man is probably here for a perfectly good reason. The first thing we're going to do is ring the doorbell."

Tristan looked horrified. "You might scare him away!"

"Geoff, you aren't taking this seriously," Natalie complained to her stepdad.

"There's no way out of the backyard except through the side gate." Mr. Peters indicated a black gate at the side of the house. "We'll see him right away if he makes a run for it. You kids stay here." He walked up to the front door and rang the bell.

Will tugged Andi's sleeve. "Why don't we take a look around the side of the house?"

Tristan nodded. "If this guy's going to try a getaway, we need to be ready."

"You guys watch too many cop movies," Andi told him.

"We should stay here, like Mr. Peters said," Melissa added.

"My stepdad can still see us," Natalie pointed out. "We're not going through the gate, or anything. We could just take a peek."

Natalie was right. The side gate was in full view of Mr. Peters, who was still standing on the front porch. Natalie creaked open the gate and peered inside.

"He's still there," she whispered. "He's putting a ladder against the back of the house!"

"Let me take a look!" Will pushed forward to see past Natalie.

"Dad!" he cried out. "What are you doing here?"

Chapter Seven

Mr. Jacobs climbed down from the ladder. Wiping his hands on his overalls, he strode over to the gate. "Will?" he said. "I thought you were out looking for Tiger this morning."

"I don't understand," Natalie said, sounding utterly confused.

Andi didn't understand, either. If Mr. Jacobs was the catnapper, why had he taken his own cat? Maybe he stole Whiskers, and then took Tiger as a cover! How many more cats had he taken? A thousand thoughts and suspicions tumbled around her head.

"We thought, uh," Tristan stammered, "we thought that — "

Mr. Jacobs pulled a notebook out of his back pocket and jotted something down. "How's the pet finding going, you two?" he asked, glancing at Andi and Tristan. He hadn't met Natalie before, but he obviously remembered the two of them from their first visit to Will. "The Hollands want me to give them a quote for a central air-conditioning system before the hot weather kicks in," Mr. Jacobs went on, putting his notebook away. "I thought I'd take a look at the outside of the house for an initial assessment, while they're away. Is there some kind of problem?"

Everyone shook their heads. It was way too embarrassing to explain to Mr. Jacobs that they'd thought he was a cat thief!

Mr. Peters came through the side gate. "I take it you're not a thief?" he said drily, extending his hand and introducing himself to Will's dad.

"A thief?" Mr. Jacobs exclaimed. "What am I supposed to have stolen?"

"Cats," Tristan said, a little helplessly.

On cue, two beautiful Burmese cats, one a darker shade of chocolate than the other, jumped up and into a large bay window on the side of the Hollands' house. Andi held out her hand to the window, and the darker brown cat reached up to butt its head softly against the glass.

"My, what a crowd!" A woman in a tracksuit appeared in the open gate. Her face cleared when she saw Mr. Peters, and she gave Natalie a wave.

"That's the Hollands' neighbor on the other side," Natalie whispered to Andi. "Mrs. Molloy. She feeds the cats when the Hollands are away."

"Hello again, Mr. Jacobs," said Mrs. Molloy, fishing around in her tracksuit pockets until she produced a key to the back door. The cats darted from the window when they heard the keys, presumably to their food bowls. "Nearly finished with the AC estimate? I'll lock the gate when I've fed the cats, if that's okay."

Mr. Peters looked interested. "You do air-conditioning?" he said to Will's dad. "That's a coincidence. Our system was making this awful clacking noise last year. Drove us all crazy. I'll bet you get pretty booked up in the summer. Any way you'd be able to take a look for me while you're here? We're just next door."

"No problem," said Mr. Jacobs. "I'll be over as soon as I'm finished."

"Well, *that* was embarrassing," Tristan muttered as they all walked back to Natalie's house.

"You don't need to tell me," Natalie muttered back.

Will looked utterly downcast, and Andi wondered if he was upset that they'd mistaken his dad for a cat thief. But then he said sadly, "Maybe Tiger hasn't been stolen. Maybe he just didn't like us anymore and ran away."

"Cats don't run away unless they've been treated badly," Andi said. "I'm sure Tiger knows how much you love him. We'll find him soon, Will."

"At least we can cross your dad off the list of suspects," Melissa put in.

"List?" Andi sighed. "If only!" Once again, they were back to square one.

As they walked into the Peterses' hallway, which was now draped with greenery for the party, Melissa stared in dismay at the door to the dog room. It was open, and there was no sign of Jet or Buddy.

"The dogs are loose!" she groaned.

"Don't panic," Andi instructed.

They immediately started checking the rooms downstairs. Mr. Peters, who had followed them back from next door, found Buddy sniffing around his study, but there was no sign of Jet.

"Hang on, I have an idea," said Andi. She dragged Melissa toward the kitchen, figuring it was best to keep her busy while the others kept searching. "The only thing Jet's really interested in, apart from walks and stuff, is food. Real food, not rabbits," she added hastily.

There was no sign of Jet in the kitchen, but Andi heard snuffling coming from the sunroom. Natalie, Tristan, and Will came running when Andi called, and together they rushed into the room to see Jet's black rump sticking out from underneath the wicker couch. His tail was wagging so fast, it was a blur against Mrs. Peters's tasteful pink-and-green furnishings. He'd obviously found something very good under the couch. Melissa turned white.

Natalie crouched down and looked underneath. "It's okay, he doesn't have Rascal! He just wants the bowl of food."

They pulled the couch away from the wall, and Natalie grabbed Jet by the collar. Once again, the little dish was tipped over and rabbit food was scattered across the tiles. It all looked horribly familiar.

"Oh, no." Andi gulped. "What if it was Jet who ate the food yesterday?"

There was a pause as this sank in.

"It means we could have been following a false trail," Tristan said at last.

Andi didn't dare look at Melissa. How would she react to yet another piece of bad news?

"But if Rascal never made it as far as the sunroom,

she might not have gone outside after all!" Melissa pointed out.

Andi nodded. "If it was Jet who ate the rabbit food last time, it does look like Rascal could still be inside."

"Those rabbit tooth marks in Tristan's apple are still our best clue," Natalie reminded everyone. "Jet's teeth are much bigger, and he'd never steal food from the counter. Rascal was in the kitchen sometime after she was missing, no question."

But where was she now? Andi wondered.

The doorbell rang.

"That'll be Dad," Will guessed. Sure enough, Mr. Jacobs was standing on the porch with a bag of tools slung over his shoulder. He glanced around at the decorations in the hallway. "Is someone having a party?"

Mr. Peters, who had come out of his study at the sound of the doorbell, rolled his eyes. "Don't ask," he said.

Mrs. Peters emerged from the living room, two enormous glass vases tucked underneath her arms. Her husband introduced Mr. Jacobs. "I've been meaning to get someone to come look at the air-conditioning," she said. "I heard reports of some unseasonably hot weather due at the end of the week. But there's so much to do when you're expecting more than a hundred guests! Mr. Jacobs, you and your family must come along tomorrow night!" She swept out of sight and through to the kitchen.

"More than a hundred guests?" Mr. Jacobs echoed in astonishment.

Mr. Peters said nothing.

"Aren't you looking forward to the party, Geoff?" Natalie sounded a little hurt.

"Of course," her stepdad said hastily.

"It'll be worth all the preparations," Natalie promised.

"It better be," Tristan said gloomily. "Mom's lined up a really itchy suit for me to wear."

The only formal dress in Andi's closet was a red one she'd last worn at a Christmas party two years ago. She hoped her mom didn't expect her to wear that. It was at least two sizes too small.

"Where would you like to start?" asked Mr. Peters, looking at Will's dad.

Mr. Jacobs looked up at the high ceiling in the hallway, then squatted down to peer along the baseboards. "Just looking for vents," he explained, noticing Andi's curious gaze. "I'll need to take a look at the original architect's drawings," he went on to Mr. Peters as he took an electronic gadget from his bag and swept it across the wall. Every now and then, the gadget made a little *bleep* sound. "These houses often have very complex systems, and although this tells me roughly where your pipes are, I'll need a hard copy of the plans before I can check all the vents."

"I'm sure they're around here somewhere — maybe the attic. Or my study—let's try there first." Still talking, Mr. Peters led Mr. Jacobs through to his study and shut the door.

Andi checked her watch. It was nearly eleven o'clock. "Time to look for Tiger and Whiskers, guys," she said. "Tristan, you and I can ask around Will's neighborhood. Nat, you and Melissa can take Mrs. Greenstreet's."

"But I wanted to look for Rascal," Melissa began.

"I know it's hard," said Natalie, "but if she is indoors, I promise she'll be safe a little longer. It would be really helpful to have you on the search this morning." Andi could tell she wanted to keep Melissa busy so she didn't worry herself to distraction.

"Okay," said Melissa. "But can we please look for Rascal this afternoon?"

"Sure," Natalie replied.

Mrs. Peters bustled back into the hall. This time, she was carrying silver candlesticks, two in each hand. "Would you have time to grab some dog food from Paws for Thought this afternoon, Natalie?" she asked. "I just haven't had time to get any this week."

"Sure," said Natalie.

Outside, the sun was shining weakly, though it still didn't feel much like spring. "Paws for Thought is halfway between our two locations," Andi said, "so let's split up right now and meet there in a couple of hours."

"Perfect," Natalie said. "My stepdad always tells me that the key to getting stuff done is good time management. Good luck — hope you find Tiger!"

"Same for you and Whiskers!" Andi called as Natalie and Melissa set off up the street with Jet straining to break free from his extendable leash.

Buddy sniffed his way along the sidewalk as Andi, Tristan, and Will headed in the opposite direction.

Will's mom had left a note to say that she'd been called out unexpectedly and wouldn't be back in time for the search after all. Will left his bike on the porch and followed Andi and Tristan as they searched the local streets. They saw a couple of cats that were the wrong color, snoozing on porches and, where families had gone away for Spring Break, unmowed lawns and mailboxes stuffed full. Without the accompanying noise of traffic, lawn mowers, and other normal neighborhood activity, Andi realized she'd never heard so much birdsong before.

Wherever they spotted cars in driveways or empty mailboxes, they knocked on the front door and asked if anyone had seen Tiger. One or two people recognized Will's cat, but no one had seen him within the last few days. By the time they reached the last street, Andi's feet were sore and her heart was heavy. It was tough, not turning up a single clue. She checked her watch. It was nearly one o'clock.

"Sorry, guys, but we've run out of time this morning," she sighed. "We'd better head for Paws for Thought or the others will wonder where we are."

Natalie, Melissa, and Jet were waiting for them when they reached the pet store. Andi took one look at the dejected way that Natalie was leaning against the pet-store window and knew they hadn't had any luck either.

"There was hardly anyone home to ask," Natalie said. "It feels like the whole town is on vacation."

"How did Mrs. Greenstreet take the news?" asked Andi.

"She was very brave about it, but you could tell she was sad," Melissa said. "I know how that feels. Knowing your pet is out there someplace but not knowing where is awful."

"I'm not even looking forward to the party anymore,"

Natalie said gloomily. "What if all the guests scare Rascal deeper into hiding?"

It was better than thinking of Rascal outside facing a fox, Andi decided, remembering the dead bird. But she didn't want to upset Melissa, so she said nothing.

When they went into the pet store, Christine's friendly cocker spaniel, Max, ambled over to greet them. Jet and Buddy followed him to his favorite spot in the window and plopped down as if their paws were tired out from all the searching.

Christine Wilson was talking to a couple and their little boy, who looked about six years old. "You'll need a warm basket, two litter boxes, and I would recommend this brand of cat food," she was saying, holding a can. "I'd keep the cat indoors for several days, just until he gets used to his new surroundings."

Andi's ears pricked up. A cat with a new home? Christine wasn't recommending kitten food, so it was clearly an adult cat.

With a meaningful glance at Andi, Tristan walked up to the counter.

"Hello, Christine," he said. He smiled at the customers. "Did I hear you talking about a new cat?"

"That's right," said the man. He was tall and broad-

shouldered with pale blond hair. "Do you have a cat, too?"

Tristan nodded. "She's a silver tabby called Lucy."

"Tabbies are gorgeous," the little boy's mother agreed.

Andi felt a flicker of excitement. Did that mean their new cat was a tabby, too? If so, it could match Tiger's description!

"Did your cat, uh, just turn up one day?" Tristan asked casually.

"Tristan," Christine said. Andi noticed a touch of steel in her voice. "Would you go get me a box of budgie treats from the storeroom?"

Tristan looked surprised. "What, now?"

"Yes, now," Christine said firmly. "I'll just be a moment," she said to her customers. "Feel free to browse the pet beds."

"Uh-oh," Andi muttered, following Christine and Tristan to the back of the store. Natalie, Melissa, and Will pressed close behind her.

Christine was standing in the storeroom with her hands on her hips. "I won't let you badger my customers!"

Tristan looked mutinous. "I was doing some important detective work!" he argued. "We're looking for two adult cats. I overheard them talking about taking in an adult cat. It's natural to ask questions!"

Christine folded her arms. "You weren't asking questions," she said. "You were laying traps. The Donaldsons got their cat from an elderly man who's going into a retirement home. I arranged for them to give the cat a new home."

"Oh," said Tristan.

"We didn't mean to upset your customers," Andi said quickly. "We're just running out of ideas on how to find Tiger and Whiskers."

"I'm sorry to hear they're still missing, really I am, but I don't think you'll track them like this." Christine ushered them all out of the storeroom. "I promise I'll let you know if I hear of any recently adopted adult cats, okay? Now, I have to get back to work."

They bought Jet's dog food and trooped outside feeling very downcast.

Andi summoned a smile from somewhere. "This isn't the end of the search, Will," she said. "We have to go back to Natalie's now because we promised to look for Rascal this afternoon, but we'll keep looking for Tiger, too, don't worry."

Will sighed. "Call me later, okay?" he said. "I'd better

go check up on Dad and make sure no one else has mistaken him for a burglar. Thanks for everything, guys. I know you're trying your best."

He trudged away with his head down and his hands shoved in his pockets. Andi sighed. Why was pet finding always so difficult?

Back at Natalie's house, they ate a quick lunch of tuna salad before planning the next phase of Rascal tracking.

"The last clue we had was the spilled food in the sunroom," Andi said.

"And the tooth marks in my apple in the kitchen," Tristan put in.

They headed for the sunroom first. Andi checked the wicker couch itself, feeling along the underside and the arms in case a tuft of rabbit fur had caught in the weave. When they found nothing, they returned to the kitchen. The food that Melissa had put out earlier was untouched.

Tristan picked up an apple and weighed it in his hand. "I've just had a weird thought," he said. "How did Rascal get that apple?"

Andi frowned. "What do you mean?"

Tristan indicated the fruit bowl, which was sitting on the counter. "The fruit bowl was up here. I know rabbits can jump, but could a rabbit really jump all the way up here from the floor?"

"Could Rascal have used the kitchen chairs?" Natalie suggested.

Melissa shook her head. "Even the chairs are too high for her."

It was a puzzle. Andi checked the rest of the gray marble countertops, working her way steadily around the kitchen. There was a bowl of freshly washed lettuce standing by the sink. A single leaf had fallen from the bowl and was sitting temptingly on the drainboard. Either this lettuce leaf had frilly edges — or something had been nibbling on it.

"Guys!" Andi called, her heart suddenly beating faster. "Take a look at this!"

Melissa grabbed the leaf and stared at it. "Rascal's been here again!"

"This is impossible," Andi said in frustration. How had Rascal gotten from the game room to the countertops in the kitchen? And how could she be moving around the house without anyone seeing her?

Chapter Eight

Apart from the nibbled lettuce leaf, there were no other clues in the kitchen.

"Melissa, where else did you leave food?" Andi asked.

"I put salad leaves in the bathroom and the living room downstairs, and the game room and Nat's room upstairs."

"Let's start in the downstairs bathroom," Tristan suggested. "It's closest to the kitchen."

They piled into the small bathroom and shut the door. Then, with mounting excitement, they stared at the piece of lettuce Melissa had left below the sink. Half of it was missing.

"Rascal's been in here, too!" Andi exclaimed.

"So where is she now?" Natalie said, staring around the empty room.

"Quit pushing," Tristan grumbled. "I'm squashed against the bathtub."

Melissa squeaked. "Natalie, you're pressing me into the towel bar!"

Andi opened the frosted glass door to the shower cubicle and stepped inside. It was a relief to find a bit of space. "Okay, it's a little small to have all of us in here," she said. "You guys check in here for gaps or holes. Tristan and I will go look in the living room."

Tristan wiped his forehead as he and Andi slipped back into the hall. Mr. and Mrs. Peters were in the living room discussing table plans for the party. They looked up as Andi and Tristan ran in and shut the door swiftly behind them.

"Rascal's left a food trail!" Andi said. "She's definitely been in the kitchen and the downstairs bathroom." She looked around and spotted another lettuce leaf under the window. Unlike the one in the bathroom, this leaf was intact.

"Rascal's been in both the kitchen *and* the downstairs bathroom?" Mrs. Peters echoed in surprise. "How has no one seen her?"

"We've been wondering the same thing," Tristan admitted. "Somehow she's sneaking around the house totally unseen."

Mrs. Peters stood up and pushed the table plan to one side. "Come on, Geoff, let's start looking," she declared. "I don't want Rascal popping out of the wood-work during the speeches. It would be far too distract-ing. Andi, have you checked the top cabinets in the kitchen yet?"

Andi shook her head. "Just the food cabinet and the cabinet with saucepans," she said.

"I'll take a look myself," Mrs. Peters offered. She cocked her head. "Can you hear a cell phone?"

Andi recognized her cell ringing faintly from the hall. She rushed out and grabbed it from her jacket pocket.

"Hello? Is this Andi?"

"Hello, Mrs. Greenstreet," Andi said, recognizing the woman's voice. "Is there any news about Whiskers?"

"I've been out with my neighbor this afternoon — she's the one who helps with my shopping and other chores. We've covered several more streets," Mrs. Greenstreet replied. "We met a number of very friendly cats along the way, but none of them *felt* quite right."

"I know what you mean," Andi said. "Buddy's coat feels like nothing else on earth. I'd know him just by the rough patch between his shoulders."

"I do miss her." Mrs. Greenstreet sounded sad. "It's silly, I know, but my armchair doesn't feel right now that Whiskers isn't sitting next to me. I've started sitting on the couch instead."

Andi looked up as Natalie and Melissa came clattering down the stairs. Natalie waved her arms and mouthed something at Andi. "Um, Mrs. Greenstreet?" Andi said, "will you excuse me for a moment?" She covered the receiver with her hand and raised her eyebrows at Natalie.

"Invite Mrs. Greenstreet to the party!" Natalie said out loud. "You never know — one of the guests might have seen Whiskers."

Andi went back to the phone. "Natalie wants to ask if you're busy tomorrow night, Mrs. Greenstreet."

"Well, no." Mrs. Greenstreet sounded surprised by the question.

"Would you like to come to a party?" Andi asked. "At Natalie's house? You can meet some more of your neighbors, and maybe we could ask if anyone has seen Whiskers in their yards or garages. There are more than a hundred guests coming."

"Good gracious! We could ask plenty of questions, couldn't we?"

"You'll have a captive audience," Andi agreed, encouraged by the lift in the old lady's voice. "So, will you come? The ASPCA veterinarian, Fisher Pearce, lives near you, so I could ask him to pick you up."

"Yes, I know Fisher," said Mrs. Greenstreet. "That would be lovely, thank you. I'll be there."

"Thanks for the suggestion, Nat," Andi said, clicking the phone shut. "Are you sure your mom won't mind?"

Natalie shrugged. "What's one more guest when we've already got so many?"

In the kitchen, Mrs. Peters was studying the leaves of a potted plant with a puzzled expression on her face.

"Doesn't that plant usually live above the plate rack, Mom?" Natalie asked.

"Yes," Mrs. Peters said with a frown, turning the pot in her hands. "It's very peculiar. Look at this." She showed them the leaves of the plant. They had very clearly been nibbled.

"Rascal!" Melissa squeaked, staring at the nibbled leaves in excitement.

Andi stared up at the shelf above the plate rack. It was a long way from the floor. "How did Rascal get up on that shelf?" she said in confusion.

"Rascal's a terrific jumper," Melissa said proudly.

"She'd need to be a terrific pole-vaulter to get way up there," Tristan pointed out.

Mrs. Peters pulled off the nibbled leaves and set the plant back on its shelf. "Why don't we leave out more lettuce tonight?" she suggested. "I'm sure we can spare some. Even a bit of radicchio, if that would help."

"Great idea, Mom," said Natalie, and she told her about inviting Mrs. Greenstreet to the party.

"What a lovely idea," said Mrs. Peters. She glanced at her husband, who was reading the paper at the kitchen table. "You don't mind, do you, Geoff?"

"Nothing to do with me," Mr. Peters grunted.

Mrs. Peters looked shocked. "It's everything to do with you, Geoff! It's *your* party!"

Mr. Peters glanced at Andi and raised his eyebrows ever so slightly. Andi had to suppress a giggle. The party on Friday night might *technically* be for Mr. Peters's birthday, but it was pretty clear who the real host was.

Andi and Tristan were surprised to find Tristan's parents were both home early.

"Hey, guys!" Tristan called, putting his keys on the hall table and bending down to pet Lucy, who was winding around his ankles and purring loudly.

"We thought we'd make an effort to be back for dinner tonight," Mrs. Saunders said, coming out of the kitchen. "We couldn't go away for Spring Break this year because we're so busy in the office, but we've hardly seen you or Dean or Andi, and half the week is gone already! Chili is on the stove, and homemade cornbread is in the oven."

As the entire Saunders family, plus Andi, sat down for dinner, Andi thought how nice it was being in the middle of a big family for a change. She loved living with her mom, but their mealtimes were never this lively. Buddy snoozed by her ankles, his head on her feet as usual.

Tristan was updating Dean and his parents on their latest pet-finding problems. "Both cats and the rabbit are still missing." He sighed. "It feels like we haven't gotten anywhere, and we've been searching all week."

"I'm sorry, Tristan," said his mom. "It must be really frustrating."

"I could drive you around Orchard Park tomorrow," Mr. Saunders offered. "Our assistant is managing the office, and I don't have anything else planned."

"Oh, yes, you do!" Mrs Saunders waved her fork at her husband. "Sorry, Tris, but I need your father tomorrow. The yard looks like a jungle, and I need him to dig out the flower beds — if we can find them. By the time we've finished, we'll have the neatest yard on the block."

"That won't be hard," joked Dean, reaching across for the last piece of cornbread. "Everyone else has abandoned theirs for Spring Break. Hey!" Tristan had beaten him to the cornbread, placing it triumphantly in the middle of his plate.

"Oh!" Andi gave a little gasp.

Tristan looked at her in surprise. "What?"

"We've been looking at this all wrong," Andi said excitedly. "People go away at Spring Break, right? So, what if Tiger or Whiskers — or both — have gotten themselves locked in a garage or a shed or something? No one would be around to let them out. We've been asking all the people who *haven't* gone on vacation about Tiger and Whiskers, when we should be checking the garages and sheds of the people who *have*!"

"So we aren't looking for thieves anymore?" Tristan asked. He looked a little disappointed.

"We should still consider that possibility," Andi said. "But this seems more likely, don't you think?"

"You're right!" Tristan spun around to his mom. "Can we go check tonight?" he pleaded. "Oakley Avenue isn't too far, and — "

"Tomorrow," Mrs. Saunders said gently. "It's past seven-thirty and too dark now."

"First thing tomorrow?" Tristan pressed.

"Okay. On one condition."

Tristan looked wary. "What?"

His mother reached for the cornbread on his plate. "That I can have this," she said, and she popped it in her mouth before Tristan could protest.

* * *

The morning of the birthday party dawned bright and warm. It looked like the unseasonably warm weather Mrs. Peters had mentioned was starting just in time. After Andi had made a call to Fisher asking him to give Mrs. Greenstreet a ride to the party that night, she and Tristan headed over to Oakley Avenue once more.

"We need to look for *empty* houses this time," Andi said. "Unswept paths, overflowing mailboxes, that kind of thing. I'll call Nat and arrange to meet at her house. We could do another split search, like before."

But Natalie and Melissa weren't going anywhere. "Rascal's been in my stepdad's study!" Natalie told Andi. "Mom put some radicchio in there last night, and it was half-eaten this morning. Don't ask how the rabbit got in there. My stepdad swears he left the door closed all night."

Nighttime, Andi thought, as she dialed Will's number to tell him about the new search. *Maybe Rascal's moving around in the dark, when everyone's asleep?* Maybe they should plan a sleepover and stake out the house in the dark.

Mr. Jacobs answered the phone and told them that Will had an orthodontist appointment that morning and wouldn't be able to help. Without Natalie, Melissa, or

Will, Andi and Tristan faced a long day of searching on their own, but it didn't stop them.

They decided to start with Whiskers and Mrs. Greenstreet.

"The garages are around the back of the houses, here," Andi said, showing Tristan the map as they stood on Mrs. Greenstreet's porch. "If you go around that way while I take this path, and we spiral outward like this" — she swirled her finger in an expanding circle around the map — "we'll meet at this point here." She indicated a large house on a corner plot. "Remember to check for signs — "

" — of unoccupied houses, yes, I know." Tristan flapped his hand at her impatiently as he started down the road.

Andi ran after him and thrust a bunch of Pet Finders Club flyers in his hand. "Just in case the neighbors want to know what you're doing," she reminded him. Then she set off down the overgrown path that ran alongside Mrs. Greenstreet's house and into a quiet alley lined with garages.

Half the garages had low windows, so that Andi could see there was no cat inside. The rest seemed very quiet when she knocked lightly for a meow in response. The sheds were all silent and locked securely. Determined to pace herself and not overlook anything, Andi moved slowly down the garages, then turned back and did the same on the other side of the lane. After a while, the garages and sheds started to blur into one another, until she felt like she was checking the same ones twice.

"Absolutely nothing," Tristan reported bleakly when they met up. "Except for an old man who threatened to set his dog on me until I produced one of our flyers and explained what I was looking for. You?"

"The same, minus the old guy with a dog." Andi sighed.

They walked despondently back to Oakley Avenue. Even the bright sunshine and unseasonable warmth did nothing to cheer them up. Andi stopped to peer over the fence of an empty house while Buddy sniffed at the bottom of the posts.

"The family's not at home!" a voice called to them from across the street. "Can I help?"

Andi turned and saw Mrs. Olson watching them from her front porch. Beside her stood a little girl about four years old.

"You're Will's friends, aren't you?" said Mrs. Olson. "Are you still looking for that cat?" Andi nodded. "I wondered what you were up to, peeking through the Mancinis' hedge. You can't be too careful at this time of year. Burglars love to find a street full of empty houses."

"Meow," said the little girl, and she ducked behind her mom's legs.

"Good little kitty," Mrs. Olson said, stroking her daughter's head and winking at Andi and Tristan. "We've just been to visit Katie's grandma," she explained. "She has a Siamese cat, and Katie's been pretending to be a cat ever since."

The little girl peeped out from behind her mom's legs and meowed again. Tristan meowed back, making her giggle.

"Do you think your neighbors would mind if we checked their sheds and garages?" Andi asked.

"Go ahead," Mrs. Olson said. "If anyone asks what you're up to, tell them I'll vouch for you, okay? Good luck." She turned and went back into the house.

Katie stayed on the porch. She pointed to the empty house where Andi had been looking over the fence. "Meow," she said again, looking hopefully at Tristan.

"Woof woof," Tristan barked, and the little girl shrieked with laughter.

"Kitty run away!" she squealed. "Naughty dog!" She pointed again at the empty house. "Grandma's cat," she said.

Next to the shuttered house, a shed was tucked into a

corner of the front yard. It was almost hidden beneath a tangle of brambles, and it was clear it hadn't been used for a long time.

"Your grandma lives there?" Andi said.

Katie shook her head. "Grandma's cat," she said.

"Your grandma's cat?" Andi said, looking again at the shuttered house with the abandoned shed. "Did you hear your grandma's cat over there, Katie?"

"Woof!" Tristan barked again, and the little girl giggled and ran inside.

"Tris!" Andi said, annoyed. "Why did you do that? I was asking Katie a serious question!"

"It was just a game," Tristan protested.

"Shh!" Andi said suddenly, tilting her head to one side and starting across the street.

"What's your problem?" asked Tristan grumpily.

Andi turned to him when they reached the yard of the shuttered house. "Katie's been hearing a cat all right," she said in excitement. "But not a Siamese like her grandma's. Siamese cats meow almost like they're talking — like a human baby cry. It's unmistakable. But listen to that!"

In the silence, they both heard a scrabbling sound from deep inside the darkened shed, followed by a long, wailing, very typical meow.

Chapter Nine

Andi plastered herself against the shed, her ear to the wood. Sensing their excitement, Buddy yipped and capered around her feet.

"Aren't we trespassing?" Tristan panted, as he pressed his own ear to the shed.

"Mrs. Olson said she'd vouch for us if anyone asked," Andi said, looping Buddy's leash around a heavy flowerpot nearby to leave her hands free. She stared up at a small window near the roof of the shed, which was loosely propped open at the top. There was a small gap between the window and the frame. Andi jumped up at the gap, trying to avoid the brambles around the base of the shed.

"There's definitely a cat in there!" she declared.

Tristan grabbed the door handle. "Locked," he said,

twisting it left, then right. They both heard the cat meow again inside the shed.

"Is there any way we can get through the window?" Tristan asked, staring at the dusty pane of glass above their heads.

"It's too small," Andi replied. "Besides, we'd scratch ourselves to death on those brambles if we fell." She spotted a tree with sturdy branches hanging over the shed. "The cat must have jumped in through the window from one of those branches. I'll bet there's nothing inside, to help it jump out again," she guessed.

Tristan tried tugging at the door of the shed again.

"Kick it," Andi suggested.

"We don't want to break it!" Tristan protested. "Mrs. Olson won't vouch for us doing that. Anyway, we'd scare the cat. Let's call my dad."

Andi frowned. "How is your dad going to help us open the door?"

"My folks keep hundreds of different keys for all their properties. Maybe he'll have one that fits."

Mr. Saunders promised he'd come over as fast as he could. "He sounded pretty hopeful," Andi commented, snapping her cell phone shut.

"I guess releasing cats from sheds beats digging

flower beds," said Tristan, squinting up at the sun. "Especially now that it's getting warm."

They settled down with their backs against the shed door. Andi made soothing sounds and sang little songs through the door to the trapped cat, in case it was frightened. Buddy whined when he heard her voice and tugged at his leash, so Andi shifted around so she could stroke his tummy at the same time.

Mr. Saunders arrived in less than ten minutes. After parking the car, he jumped out carrying a bag that jingled loudly. "I brought as many as I could find," he said, dumping the contents of the bag on the grass beside the shed. He picked a small bronze key from the pile and tried to fit it in the lock. He jiggled it around, but it wouldn't go in all the way.

There was a frantic scrabbling sound on the other side of the door. If it was one of the missing cats, it had been shut in that shed for most of the week and would be very hungry, maybe even traumatized.

"Try this one, Dad," Tristan suggested, handing over a slightly smaller key. Mr. Saunders tried again, leaning his head against the door to listen for the telltale click of an opening lock.

"It's like robbing a bank," Tristan said as his dad discarded the second key and chose a third.

"Except we're not stealing anything, we're setting something free," Andi reminded him.

"This isn't working," Mr. Saunders sighed, straightening up from his fourth attempt on the lock. "It looks like we have to get the real key from somewhere."

"Looking for these?"

They turned to see Mrs. Olson standing in the driveway behind them, dangling a key ring between her fingers.

"Perfect!" Andi gasped.

"The Mancinis always leave a set of keys with me when they go away," Mrs. Olson said, fiddling with the key ring. "When Katie came inside and told me about the game she'd been playing with you, I figured maybe you'd found something." She detached the smallest key and handed it to Andi. "Try this," she suggested.

Andi put the key in the lock and carefully turned it. There was a smooth clicking sound. Cautiously, she turned the handle and tugged the door open. A golden blur shot out.

Andi leaped to her feet and flung herself on the frightened cat, pinning it to the grass, where it struggled and spat beneath her.

"Shh. It's okay . . . " she said soothingly, trying to

avoid the cat's flashing claws. At last she managed to get a firm grip and started stroking the cat's head. The cat stopped struggling, but its ears were still flat on its head as if it was waiting for its chance to escape. It was dusty, but its tabby markings and white tummy were clear. Gorgeous golden tabby stripes stretched along its body. There was no sign of a collar.

"It's pretty fat for a cat that's gone without food for a couple of days," Mr. Saunders remarked. "And it doesn't look like it's been hurt. Do you think it's one of the cats you've been looking for?"

Andi checked the cat over. "It's a tom," she said. "And Will did say that Tiger was fat." She gazed in delight at the cat in her arms. They had found Tiger! Will was going to be so pleased!

Tristan unwrapped his jacket, which he'd tied to his waist, and folded it around the cat to stop it from struggling. "Let's go see if Will's home!"

"It'll be time for the party soon," Mr. Saunders reminded them as he climbed back into his car. "You're both sleeping over at Natalie's, right?"

The party! Andi had forgotten all about it. It was already past four o'clock, and the party started at seven. Her mom was coming home at six, and she had to get back and change and —

"Earth to Andi!" Tristan's voice interrupted her thoughts. "Let's go reunite Will with Tiger!"

"We have to do it fast," said Andi.

They were so excited, it was hard not to run up the road, but Andi and Tristan walked as carefully as they could to avoid scaring Tiger any more. Tristan held his jacket like it contained fragile glass as Andi rang the bell.

There was no answer.

"They must still be at the orthodontist," Andi realized. "What should we do? We can't leave Tiger here. He's hungry and scared. He could run off again."

"Let's take him back to Natalie's," Tristan suggested. "The Jacobses are coming to the party tonight, aren't they? We can reunite them there."

Andi called home to leave a message for her mom, explaining that she was going straight over to Natalie's house and asking her mom to bring her party outfit and overnight bag. Andi's heart sank as she realized she'd have to wear her red dress from two years ago. She'd been so busy looking for Rascal, Whiskers, and Tiger that she hadn't had a chance to look for a new outfit.

The Peterses' house was almost unrecognizable. Twinkling white lights were strung around the front of the house, and a wreath of spring flowers and gold-sprayed branches hung on the door. Men in blue overalls were carrying tables and chairs and boxes of bottled beverages into the house from a row of vans parked outside. Tristan held Tiger carefully as he and Andi picked their way through the bustle of party preparations in the hallway.

"You've found Tiger!" Natalie recognized the beautiful striped tabby at once. "That's fantastic! But why have you brought him here?"

"Will and his folks weren't at home," Andi explained. "Can we put Tiger someplace where he'll be safe?"

"How about my bedroom?" Natalie suggested, stroking the cat's soft, furry head.

Tristan took Tiger upstairs while Andi put Buddy in the dog room with Jet. The terrier immediately curled up next to the black Labrador, who barely raised his head as Andi pulled the door shut. It looked like the dogs were getting used to the new Rascal routine.

"Where's Melissa?" Andi asked as they made their way upstairs with a bowl of water and a can of sardines for Tiger. The banisters had been wrapped in ivy, and it felt a little like climbing a tree.

"Staking out the game room again," Natalie replied. "I'm getting pretty worried about her, actually. I can't even get her interested in her party outfit."

"I wouldn't be able to think about a party outfit if Rascal were *my* pet," Andi admitted.

Natalie looked crushed. "I know what you mean," she said, "but it's such a great outfit — we found it at the mall the other day. It's this gorgeous little turquoise . . ." She stopped herself. "Anyway, you'd think it might cheer her up a little. I don't think Rascal's going to come out tonight, anyway, not with all these people around."

They found Tristan in Natalie's bedroom, brushing dust and cobwebs out of Tiger's fur. "Do you think Melissa will mind me using Rascal's grooming brush?" he asked.

"Probably," Natalie said tartly, reaching down to take the brush away from Tristan, "if it *was* Rascal's grooming brush. But it's my hairbrush."

Melissa came into the bedroom. She stopped dead at the sight of Tiger drinking thirstily from the bowl of water. "What's that cat doing in here?" she asked abruptly. "What if Rascal sees him?"

Andi stopped wrestling with the can of sardines. She hadn't considered that. It was getting more and more complicated, keeping all these animals away from each other.

"We'll put him in the garage," Natalie decided, as

Tiger started meowing hopefully at the smell of sardines. "Besides, he might get scared with all the people in the house tonight."

They paraded back downstairs, with Tristan carrying Tiger again. Mrs. Peters was straightening a floral arrangement on the hall table. "Andi, I spoke to your mother," she said. "She got home about twenty minutes ago, and she's coming straight over with your outfit, okay? Oh!" she exclaimed when she finally looked up from the arrangement. "Is that a cat?"

Natalie explained about Tiger. "We thought he could go in the garage, just until his owners arrive," she said.

Mrs. Peters looked relieved. "Yes, the garage would be good," she said. "I don't think we could cope with another animal in the house tonight." She fanned herself with an elegantly manicured hand. "It's warming up, isn't it?" she said. "Rather pleasant for this time of year, but with a house full of people this evening, we might need to turn on the air-conditioning a little earlier than usual. It would be great if Geoff could get it fixed before our guests arrive. Mr. Jacobs is coming soon, so maybe he'll have some ideas. What do you think of these flowers, Natalie? Are they a little . . . too floral?"

"Isn't that what flowers are? Floral?" Tristan whispered to Andi as they left Natalie and Melissa with Mrs.

Peters and took Tiger through the inside door to the garage. Andi bit her lip to keep from giggling.

"Will was right about Tiger liking sardines," she commented, watching the golden tabby devour the bowl of fish they had put on the floor. "I don't think he's even chewing them!"

"I hope Rascal doesn't turn up in here tonight," Tristan said. "Tiger would terrify her."

"We'll keep the door shut tight," Andi decided.

"That doesn't seem to help," Tristan pointed out. "Remember how Rascal got into Mr. Peters's study, even though he closed the door?"

"Well, it's the best we can do," Andi said firmly. "Until we figure out how Rascal does it, we just have to do the logical thing and shut the doors."

Tiger finished the sardines and sat down with his tail curled neatly over his paws. He looked up at Andi and Tristan with his gorgeous amber eyes and opened his mouth in a loud meow.

"Feeling a little better?" Tristan asked. "Hey, Andi, remember how Will said he loved playing with that toy mouse?" He found a roll of string on a shelf and waved the end in front of Tiger. The tabby pounced, his long striped tail whisking back and forth as he chased the string across the floor. "You'll be home with your own mousie soon, old guy," Tristan promised, bending down to smooth Tiger's fur.

Andi couldn't help thinking about Mrs. Greenstreet's gentle cat, Whiskers, still lost somewhere in Orchard Park. She hoped their luck would hold out long enough to find her, too.

They left Tiger on a folded blanket in a corner of the garage. Then Tristan headed home to change while Andi went to look at the dining room. It was draped in white, yellow, and gold fabric, and sprays of white flowers sat in the middle of the long table on the far side of the room. Amid several tempting plates of appetizers, Mr. Peters's birthday cake took pride of place on a golden stand, with curly white ribbons tumbling artistically from the top of the frosting. It looked very striking, but Andi wondered how much of it was what Mr. Peters would like. It was his birthday, after all.

"Hi there! Did you miss me?"

Andi whirled around to see her mom standing in the doorway, wearing a shimmery lilac dress. "Mom!" she cried, rushing over to give her mother a hug. "How was the conference?"

Mrs. Talbot hugged her back. "Useful, but dull," she said. "I would much rather have been home with you and Buddy. Mind you, from what I hear, I wouldn't have seen you much, with all the pet finding you've been do-ing this week. So, are you going to get changed now?"

"Mom," Andi began, as she followed her mom out of the dining room, "about my outfit. I don't think I fit into it anymore."

"How do you know?" teased Mrs. Talbot, leading Andi into the den. "You haven't even seen it yet."

Andi clapped her hands with delight when she saw the clothes laid across the couch. There was a pair of blue satin cargo pants, cropped just below the knee, and a stretchy, long-sleeved blue top decorated with a wave of plain white crystals. Blue flats stood on the floor. "It's *gorgeous*!" she said when she could speak. "Thank you so much, Mom!"

"Quick, go upstairs and put it on," said Mrs. Talbot, smiling.

Andi hugged her again, hard, before running upstairs to change. If only they'd managed to find Rascal and Whiskers, this party would have been perfect!

Chapter Ten

Among the first guests to arrive, on the dot of seven o'clock, were the Jacobses. Mr. Peters promptly dragged Mr. Jacobs to his study to talk about the air-conditioning.

Andi, feeling fantastic in her new clothes, rushed up to Will. "You won't believe it," she grinned at him, "but Tiger's here!"

Will looked astonished. "You mean, in this house?"

"Yup, right here," Tristan confirmed, appearing behind Andi.

Natalie and Melissa joined them as they led Will to the garage. Melissa looked pale and sad, but Andi was pleased to see Natalie had persuaded her to put on her party clothes. The turquoise dress suited her and brought out a little color in her cheeks.

Will pushed open the door to the garage and rushed

inside. There was a deep, rumbling meow of a welcome and the sound of a cat jumping lightly down from the workbench.

"Tiger!" Will scooped up the purring tabby cat and held him close. "It's really you!"

Andi felt her eyes tearing up.

"Thank you so, so much!" Will said, looking over Tiger's head at the Pet Finders. "Mom and Dad will be totally amazed that you found him. Where was he?"

Andi and Tristan took turns describing Tiger's dramatic rescue. Aware of how Melissa must be feeling, Andi was careful to keep the story short. She had to step on Tristan's toe every now and then to stop him from embellishing it too much. She could imagine what it was like for Melissa, seeing Will so happy when she was still feeling so miserable about Rascal.

They left Will to get reacquainted with Tiger and wandered back through the house. Nearly all the guests had arrived by now and were standing around in their best evening clothes, talking and laughing and holding crystal glasses. The Thai-style appetizers were disappearing fast; Andi caught sight of Tristan watching mournfully as a woman with long scarlet fingernails took the last dumpling.

"Your suit's not so bad," Andi said, looking critically at Tristan.

Tristan grimaced and tugged at his shirt collar. "It's very itchy."

"You almost look human," Natalie said kindly, picking an imaginary piece of fluff off her floaty sapphire-colored dress.

Mrs. Peters rushed up to them, magnificent in full-length red satin. "Natalie, have you seen your step-father? Everyone's here, but there's no sign of him."

"From Pet Finding to People Finding," Tristan said promptly, dragging his gaze away from the empty plate. "We'll find him, Mrs. Peters. Don't worry."

"I got the impression your stepdad wasn't looking for-ward to the party," Andi whispered to Natalie as they squeezed through the crowded downstairs rooms look-ing for the guest of honor. "Maybe he's run away."

"He wouldn't do that," Natalie decided. "He knows it would cause *way* too much trouble with my mom. Uh, Tris? My stepdad wouldn't be in the broom closet."

Tristan reversed out of the closet and dusted down his jacket. "Sorry," he said. "I went into pet-finding mode there."

"Was there any sign of Rascal in there?" asked Melissa. "I put some lettuce leaves behind the door earlier."

Tristan shook his head. "Sorry, there were some leaves, but they didn't look like they'd been eaten."

They kept hunting for Mr. Peters. It felt different to be searching for a person in Natalie's house instead of a rabbit. Andi resisted the urge to block off all the small spaces they passed.

As they turned the corner on the upstairs landing, there was an odd thumping noise above their heads.

Tristan looked up at the ceiling. "What's up there, Nat?"

"Just the attic," Natalie said. "But my stepdad wouldn't — "

They turned the corner and came face-to-face with Mr. Peters and Mr. Jacobs descending the attic ladder. Mr. Peters looked happier than he had all week.

"Geoff!" cried Natalie. "Your suit! Mom's going to totally kill you!"

Mr. Peters looked down at his cobwebby tuxedo and picked off a couple of dead spiders that were dangling from the hem of his jacket. "Since we were upstairs, I asked Mr. Jacobs about installing AC in the attic," he said, looking sheepish. "I've been thinking of converting it into a bedroom. It's a terrific space, and . . . anyway, what have I missed?"

Natalie dragged her stepfather to the nearest

bathroom. "You almost missed all the appetizers!" she said disapprovingly, sponging down his tuxedo before bustling him down the stairs.

"You'll be lucky to find any dumplings," Tristan grumbled under his breath as he and Andi followed.

Over the heads of the guests gathered in the hallway, Andi saw Mrs. Greenstreet standing on the porch with Fisher Pearce and Christine Wilson.

Andi ran downstairs to give them the good news. "We found Tiger! Will's with him now, in the garage. Fisher, do you think you could quickly check him over, to make sure he's okay?"

"You found Tiger?" Mrs. Greenstreet sounded pleased. "That's very good news. Will must be delighted."

"Yes, he is. We found Tiger in a locked shed," Andi explained, letting Mrs. Greenstreet take her arm. She led the new arrivals through the crowds. "Now that we know what to look for — houses where people have gone *away* for Spring Break — we'll start searching for Whiskers again tomorrow, in case the same thing happened to her."

Christine took Mrs. Greenstreet through to the kitchen while Andi escorted Fisher to the garage. They found Will sitting cross-legged on the floor. Tiger was standing on his hind legs, batting at the piece of string.

He looked pretty fit for a cat who'd been stuck in a shed.

"Will, this is Fisher," Andi began.

Suddenly, there was a loud scrabbling noise inside the door to the house. To Andi's horror, two wet black noses shoved the door wide open, sniffing eagerly. Jet and Buddy had escaped from the dog room!

"I'm so sorry!" A woman in a dark blue dress rushed up behind the dogs. "I was looking for the downstairs bathroom and accidentally let the dogs out — "

Will let out a yelp as Tiger dug his claws into his lap and then launched straight past Fisher and Andi, out of the garage and into the house. Jet and Buddy whirled around and hurtled away in pursuit.

"Quick!" Andi yelled.

Tiger streaked through the kitchen with Jet and Buddy hot on his tail. With one monumental effort, Andi flung herself at Jet and snuck a finger through his collar, bringing him to a screeching halt in the doorway to the sunroom. Will skidded to a halt just behind her. Meanwhile, Fisher scooped Buddy up with one hand.

Mrs. Greenstreet was sitting on the wicker couch with Tiger trembling in her arms.

"Thanks, Mrs. Greenstreet!" Andi panted. "If Tiger had made it into the backyard, we could have lost him again!"

Mrs. Greenstreet ran her hand over the terrified, fluffed-up cat. "Tiger?" she echoed. "This isn't Tiger. It's Whiskers!"

"No, this is my cat, Tiger," Will said.

"Tristan and I found him today," Andi added.

Mrs. Greenstreet shook her head. With her fingers, she gently followed the contours of Tiger's ears. "I promise you this is Whiskers," she said calmly.

A cheer went up from inside the dining room. Andi guessed Mr. Peters had made his entrance at last. Tristan, Natalie, and Melissa came out of the dining room and walked through the kitchen, Natalie with her arm firmly linked through Melissa's. They all stopped in the doorway to the sunroom, clearly sensing that something was up.

"What's going on?" Tristan asked, looking around.

"Mrs. Greenstreet just told us that Tiger isn't Tiger," Fisher announced. "He's Whiskers."

Tristan opened his eyes wide in astonishment.

"But Mrs. Greenstreet, this can't be Whiskers!" Natalie protested. "Tiger's a tomcat, and you said Whiskers was a girl."

The beautiful tabby cat was sitting on Mrs. Greenstreet's lap with its eyes half-closed. There was no sign of the playful, energetic cat they'd seen in the garage

with Will. Instead, this was a very gentle pet who wasn't going to rush around and demand busy games. It was almost as if he knew Mrs. Greenstreet couldn't see and needed a special kind of stillness.

"I'd know that purr anywhere," Mrs. Greenstreet said with a smile. "I must confess, I only *assumed* Whiskers was a girl. Everyone was always telling me how pretty she was, you see. They must have figured she was a girl just from the way she — or he — looked. What a mix-up!"

Andi glanced at Will, who was looking devastated. They'd all been so sure it was Tiger — Will most of all. That was the weird part. Surely an owner wouldn't mistake the identity of his own cat?

Then, like the sun breaking through a cloud, something occurred to her. Was it possible that this cat was Tiger *and* Whiskers?

"Tristan, go get that roll of string from the garage, will you?" she said. "I have a theory I'd like to try out."

When Tristan returned with the cord, Andi took it and waved it in front of the sleepy cat. Immediately, he pricked up his ears.

"Oh!" Mrs. Greenstreet gasped as the cat leaped off her lap and raced after the cord, his claws skittering on the tiles. "Is Whiskers playing?"

"It *is* Tiger," Will said, grinning broadly. He scooped the cat off the floor and sat down next to Mrs. Greenstreet. The cat immediately rolled over on his back and started batting at Will's fingers.

Andi looked at Fisher, feeling totally confused. "Is it possible for a cat to have a split personality?"

Fisher nodded. "Cats often reflect the behavior of their owners," he said. "Will is young and energetic, while Mrs. Greenstreet leads a quieter life. It's clear that this cat loves them both equally and adjusts his behavior according to the person he's with."

Suddenly, Tiger stopped playing. He padded along the couch and nudged his head very gently against Mrs. Greenstreet's arm. As soon as the elderly lady moved her hand, the cat snuggled down beside her and rested his head on her knee. He looked as if running around was the last thing he'd want to do.

Andi watched the transformation from playful Tiger to docile Whiskers with a mixture of delight and alarm. It was fantastic to think they'd solved two cases at once, but if Tiger and Whiskers were the same cat, what were Will and Mrs. Greenstreet going to do now?

"I don't understand," Melissa said, looking from Will to Mrs. Greenstreet and back again.

"You're not the only one," Natalie muttered.

"No wonder he's so fat," Tristan declared. "You guys have both been feeding him."

Fisher leaned down and stroked Tiger gently. "Hmm," he said with a frown. "He's quite overweight. We might have to put him on a special diet. The extra weight may have helped him when he went without food for a few days, but it's very dangerous in the long term and can cause diabetes and liver disease. We'll talk about it later, Will — I mean, Mrs. Greenstreet." He broke off. "Who should I be talking to here?"

Andi was wondering the same thing. They'd never found a cat with two owners before. If Tiger and Whiskers were the same cat, who actually owned him?

"How long have you had Tiger, Will?" Mrs. Greenstreet asked.

"Nearly three years," Will replied.

"Then he *is* yours," Mrs. Greenstreet said simply. "Whiskers — Tiger, I mean — only came to me several months ago."

Will ran his hand along Tiger's back and looked thoughtful. "I don't mind sharing him," he said at last. "I mean, I've been sharing him for three months, haven't I? I just didn't know it."

"Are you sure?" Mrs. Greenstreet broke into such a delighted smile that Andi felt tears welling up in her eyes. "If you can really spare him, I would love that. I'll try to remember to call him Tiger. When Andi and Tristan told me you'd lost your cat, they said he had beautiful gold stripes. Is that where his name came from?"

"Yep," said Will. "He has a very unusual gold-and-chocolate coat."

Mrs. Greenstreet beamed. "It's lovely to be able to picture her — I mean, him — properly. My neighbor just described him as a tabby, so I had an idea in my head that he was a mix of brown and gray. I had a brown-and-gray tabby when I was younger, you see. But I'm surprised no one recognized him from your posters and realized Tiger and Whiskers were the same cat!"

"The picture on Tiger's poster was very small," Will explained. "He never stayed still long enough for me to take a photo." He grinned down at the tabby, who was lying as still as a statue on Mrs. Greenstreet's lap. "I guess he saved his quiet time for when he was with you!"

Melissa sniffed, as if she was struggling not to cry. Andi felt a wave of sympathy for her.

Mr. Peters came out of the dining room with Mr. Jacobs then.

"Where are you going now?" Natalie asked her stepdad. "You can't keep running away from your own party!"

Mr. Peters looked defensive. "We checked the vents upstairs, and we need to do the same down here. Your mom wants the air-conditioning on before we cut the cake. With so many people in the dining room, it's getting pretty stuffy."

"My stepdad is hopeless," Natalie muttered, watching them disappear. "If he gets his tux dirty again, Mom is going to be furious. He'll be gone more than half an hour, I know it. Those vents are everywhere."

Will and Mrs. Greenstreet were figuring out Tiger's feeding program. "How about you feed him in the morning, then we have him for his evening meal?" Will suggested. "Feeding him's always a rush for me in the morning because I have to get ready for school."

"Will's being so cool about this," Tristan whispered to Andi. "I could never share Lucy."

"I couldn't share Rascal, either," Melissa said miserably, overhearing. "That is, if I ever find her again."

Andi glanced around the sunroom. Where *was* that little rabbit? If only they could second-guess Rascal's next move and wait for her. How was she managing to pop up all over the house without anyone seeing her? She was small, but not that small!

As Will bent down to put his cheek against Tiger's, Melissa let out a strangled sob and rushed out of the sunroom. Andi, Natalie, and Tristan followed her up the stairs to Natalie's bedroom, where she had flung herself down on the bed.

"I've walked up and down this corridor a hundred times," she wailed. "If I just knew where Rascal was hiding, at least I could wait in the right place. She has to come out sometime, doesn't she?" She broke into a fresh storm of tears.

"Of course she does," Andi said. "You've just got to be patient." But it was hard to keep reassuring Melissa when they were no closer to solving the mystery of the disappearing — and reappearing — runaway rabbit.

Melissa blew her nose. "It's okay," she said in a small, sad whisper. "I know what you're all thinking." She swallowed. "I'm never going to see Rascal again, am I? She's gone forever, and she's not coming back."

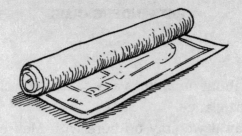

Chapter Eleven

There was a knock on the bedroom door.

"Natalie?" It was Mrs. Peters, looking flustered. "Have you seen your stepfather anywhere? I really would like the air-conditioning on in the dining room now. We can't cut the cake without the guest of honor! Honestly, you would think this was my party, not Geoff's at all. . . . " She broke off as she noticed Melissa's red eyes and blotchy face. "Oh, poor you," she said gently. "Still no news of Rascal?"

Melissa shook her head miserably. "I hope you don't mind, Mrs. Peters, but I think I'll skip dinner," she said. "I'm not very hungry."

"I'll get Maria to bring you up a plate," Mrs. Peters decided. "I'm sure there are some appetizers left."

Tristan opened his mouth as if he was about to start

muttering about dumplings again, but Andi silenced him with a fierce glance.

"Is it okay if we stay up here with Melissa?" Natalie asked. "The party's great, but Melissa needs us now."

"Of course," Mrs. Peters said, fanning herself vigorously. "But could you do me a favor first? Find your stepfather and get him to turn on the air-conditioning, even if that clacking noise is still there. Then try and get him downstairs for dinner, or he'll miss the cake altogether!" She swept out of the room, shutting the door behind her.

"Tristan and I will look for Mr. Peters," Andi decided. "He said he was going to check the vents downstairs, didn't he?"

They found Mr. Peters and Mr. Jacobs on their hands and knees in the downstairs bathroom, peering under the sink. They had taken the grille off the air-conditioning vent, and Mr. Jacobs was checking inside the flue. Andi cleared her throat, and the two men looked up.

"Sorry to interrupt," she said, "but Mrs. Peters is looking for you, Mr. Peters. She'd like you to turn on the AC, even if it's still making noise."

Mr. Peters climbed to his feet and dusted down his suit, which was looking even more crumpled than before. He picked up the plans of the house and studied them for a moment. "We've just got two more vents," he said. "One in the kitchen ceiling, and one in the sunroom."

"We found a loose-fitting valve in the study that could have been causing the noise," Mr. Jacobs added. "I tightened it up, but we do need to check all the vents in the house before I can be sure that we found the problem."

"Mrs. Peters wants to cut the cake in a few minutes," Tristan added.

Mr. Peters held up his hands in defeat. "I get the message!" he said. "We'll check these last two, switch the system on, and then come in, I promise." He glanced at his watch. "It should only take five minutes to look at these vents, so it'll be back on by eight o'clock."

Andi and Tristan checked on Jet and Buddy, who were shut back in the dog room. They were both panting with their mouths wide open when Andi and Tristan went in.

"Thank goodness Rascal never turned up in here," Andi said, scratching Buddy's tummy. "She would have gotten the fright of her life, meeting these two."

They hung up a sign on the dog-room door that read THIS IS NOT A BATHROOM — DO NOT OPEN!, in case any more guests were about to let the dogs out by mistake. Then, heading back to join Natalie and Melissa, they met

Maria on the stairs. The housekeeper was balancing a tray containing four glasses of orange soda and four plates piled high with a selection of appetizers—including several dumplings and a small pot of spicy dipping sauce.

Tristan's eyes lit up. "Fantastic!" he murmured, taking the tray from Maria. "We'll take it from here, thanks!"

"Maria?" Andi asked. "Could you please tell Mrs. Peters that the air-conditioning is going back on in five minutes? Thanks!"

"Hurry up, Andi!" Tristan called over his shoulder as he carried the tray upstairs, "or I'll eat your food as well!"

Soon they had laid out a feast on Natalie's bedroom carpet. Natalie switched off the main light and draped a set of twinkle lights around the head of her bed. They helped create a party atmosphere as Andi, Tristan, and Natalie took turns coaxing Melissa into eating something.

"Try the sticky rice balls," Natalie urged. "They're totally out of this world."

"I'm okay, thanks." Melissa gazed out of the window at the night sky and let out a heavy sigh.

"Let's get out our sleeping bags," Andi suggested, "and start this sleepover for real."

They laid the bags in a circle around the picnic spread. "It's like we're a bunch of cowboys in the desert," Tristan said, propping himself up on his elbow. He pretended to warm his hands at an imaginary campfire. "*I was bo-orn*," he began to sing in a tuneless voice, "*under a wa-a-and'rin' star . . .* "

"Shh!" Andi said. She prodded him so he fell over on his side. "You'll wake up the rattlesnake I saw back there."

Tristan fanned himself with a folded napkin as the temperature in the bedroom grew hotter. Andi stretched out to grab a spring roll. She found herself eye level with the air-conditioning vent between Natalie's and Melissa's beds and thought about how wonderful it would be to feel cool air coasting out of the vent and on to her face.

"Are Jet and Bud okay?" Natalie asked.

"Hot," Andi said. "I bet they can't wait for the AC to come on."

"They won't feel it in the dog room," Natalie said, reaching for another sticky rice ball. "There's no vent in there."

Andi dropped her spring roll.

"Don't you want that?" said Tristan hopefully.

Andi didn't reply. Instead, she scrambled to her feet

and rushed over to the air vent. The grille was fixed to the wall on a hinge, so she could lift up the mesh with one finger and peer into the darkness.

"What on earth are you doing?" said Natalie.

"The air-conditioning," Andi muttered. "Why didn't we think of that before? There are vents everywhere in the house — you said so yourself, Nat. The grilles are on hinges! Could Rascal have pushed one open and gotten inside the system?"

The others stared at her, food and drink forgotten. Even Melissa was looking up with hope flaring in her eyes.

"Are there vents in all the places where Rascal has been eating the food?" Andi prompted.

Natalie shook her head. "I don't know. But Geoff has the plans. We could go check with him."

They ran downstairs to the kitchen. There was no sign of Mr. Jacobs or Mr. Peters.

"Mr. Peters said there was a vent near the kitchen ceiling," Andi remembered, staring upward. "Remember how your mom found that nibbled plant on the shelf above the plate rack, Nat? That must have been how Rascal did it! She didn't jump up — she jumped *down*!"

"And then she must have jumped down to eat the lettuce by the sink, and jumped across to the table to reach the apple," Natalie deduced, staring around the room, "and finally jumped to the floor." They all stared at a second vent set into the baseboard. It all made perfect sense.

Tristan pounced on a scroll of pale blue paper lying on the table. "Here are the plans!"

Melissa grabbed the paper from him. "Kitchen, sunroom, downstairs bathroom, study, game room," she said, tracing her finger across the plans. "There are vents in all those rooms!"

"Rascal could have been using it as a bunch of tunnels," said Natalie, "just like she learned in your obstacle courses."

"And that's how she's moving from room to room without anyone seeing her!" Andi said in triumph.

Tristan raised his eyebrows. "Did we just solve another case?"

"Not yet," Andi warned. "But I think we're getting close."

Behind them, the kitchen clock chimed eight o'clock. Andi frowned. Someone had mentioned eight o'clock earlier, hadn't they?

"Oh, no!" she gasped. "Mr. Peters is about to turn on the system!"

Melissa went white.

"Quick, Nat, where's the switch?" Andi said.

"In the garage."

"There's no time to lose," Andi said urgently. "We have to stop them!"

They hurtled out of the kitchen and raced along the corridor. Mr. Peters and Mr. Jacobs were standing together in the garage, Mr. Jacobs cuddling Tiger and Mr. Peters's hand raised to flip the switch.

"Stop!" Andi yelled. *"Don't turn on the air-conditioning!"*

Looking astonished, Mr. Peters lowered his hand.

Natalie thrust the building plans under her step-father's nose. "We think Rascal is inside the system!"

"Mr. Jacobs, is it possible for a rabbit to travel through the air-conditioning ducts?" Andi asked.

"Well, this is an old system," he said. "The pipes are pretty narrow. But sure — a rabbit could run around in there, if it was used to small spaces."

"Rascal loves her cardboard tunnels," Melissa explained. "The air-conditioning system must have seemed like a huge playground!"

Mrs. Peters rushed into the garage with several guests behind her. "I heard a scream! Is someone hurt?"

Andi quickly explained their theory.

"So Rascal really could be inside the air-conditioning?"

Fisher said, stepping out from behind Nat's mom. "How are you going to get her out?"

"How about putting food next to each vent?" said Christine.

"How about using the dogs to flush her out?" Tristan suggested.

"Or Tiger?" Will offered.

"I wouldn't advise it," Fisher said, seeing that Melissa looked alarmed. "We don't want to scare Rascal so much that she never comes out."

All the guests started talking, until Mr. Peters called for silence by waving his arms above his head. "Where's Melissa?"

Melissa put up her hand.

"Any tips on how to get Rascal out of the tunnels?" Mr. Peters asked.

"She usually comes when I rattle some food for her," Melissa said. "But now I've seen how complicated the air-conditioning system is, I think she must have been too far down a tunnel to hear me."

"I've got an idea," Andi announced. "There are more than a hundred guests here tonight, right? How many vents are there in the house, Mr. Peters?"

"Sixteen," Mr. Peters said promptly.

"Could we put a couple of guests at each air vent?"

Andi asked. "They can listen for Rascal, and that way the whole house can be covered at the same time."

Mrs. Peters turned to her guests. "Would anyone object? As soon as we've found the rabbit, I promise we'll cut the cake."

"I'd be happy to help out," said the woman in the dark blue dress who had mistakenly let the dogs out earlier.

Melissa and Natalie took charge of assigning a vent to each pair of guests, consulting the plans to be sure every vent was covered. Tristan asked the remaining guests to patrol the corridors between the rooms, in case Rascal made a break for it. Will took Mrs. Green-street's arm to lead her to their vent, which was in the corridor leading to the garage.

Once everyone was in position, Melissa, Andi, Tristan, and Natalie started moving steadily through the house. The Pet Finders kept very quiet, so the only sound was Melissa calling Rascal's name and rattling the bowl of food. Upstairs, the guests by each vent shook their heads, indicating they hadn't heard any sign of the rabbit in the vent. Downstairs bathroom, study, kitchen, sunroom . . . still no trace of Rascal. Melissa bit her lip but kept going, although her voice was starting to tremble.

The last vent in the house was the one guarded by Will and Mrs. Greenstreet. The old lady was standing very still, with her head tilted to one side. As Andi and the others approached, she held up her hand.

"Can you hear something?" Andi whispered.

Mrs. Greenstreet nodded. "There!" she said suddenly, pointing at a section of the wall. "A scrabbling sound."

Andi listened, but she couldn't hear anything. Judging from the expressions on the faces of the others, neither could they.

"Um," Andi said, "are you sure?"

Mrs. Greenstreet smiled as she ran her fingers lightly over the wall. "My hearing has become very finely tuned since I lost my sight," she said. "Your rabbit is moving that way." She pointed back toward the hall.

"I'll stay by the vent," Will offered. "You go with the others, Mrs. Greenstreet. They need your ears."

Mrs. Greenstreet nodded and took Andi's arm. Melissa ran down the hall, rattling the box.

"Scrabbling!" Tristan squeaked, pointing upward. "I heard it! Rascal's headed upstairs!"

The guests by the downstairs vents started to appear in the hall when they heard the chase moving upstairs again. Mrs. Greenstreet led the way with a confident step: listening, listening. . . .

As Andi grew used to the tiny, soft sounds of the rabbit hopping through the pipes, she found she could track Rascal's movements more accurately. Judging from the sparkle in Melissa's eyes, so could she. Tristan and Natalie tracked Rascal's progress on the plans, moving their fingers along the mapped pipes and squabbling in hushed voices about which direction she was taking.

They followed Rascal along the landing toward one of the guest bedrooms. Andi ran ahead and held open the door so Melissa, Natalie, Tristan, and Mrs. Greenstreet could come in.

"The vent's under the window," Natalie whispered, looking up from the plans.

Melissa crouched down at the vent and rattled the food.

Come on, come on! Andi found herself willing the little rabbit along through the pipes.

The scrabbling came closer and closer. Then, just inside the vent opening, it stopped.

Melissa took a handful of sunflower seeds out of the bowl and put them in a neat pile just outside the vent. Then she sat back to wait.

A wriggling white nose peeped out. Rascal cautiously took a seed before backing into the pipe again. Soon,

she came back for another. This time, she stayed at the
entrance to the tunnel, munching the seed and looking
around with her bright black eyes. When she saw
Melissa, she lifted her head and twitched her nose.

Very slowly, Melissa reached toward her, murmuring
soothing words the whole time. Andi was really impressed at her patience. Melissa's fingers moved closer
and closer toward Rascal's fur, then gently smoothed
her ears. Rascal tensed but didn't try to run back into
the tunnel. Melissa closed her hand firmly around the
rabbit's tummy and lifted her up.

Andi shared a look of sheer triumph with Tristan.
They'd done it! "You're so clever, finding all those lettuce leaves," Melissa whispered, kissing Rascal's head
over and over. "I'm never going to lose you again, I
promise!"

The rabbit looked a little dusty, but her eyes were
clear and she didn't look too bad for her adventure
within the walls.

"Awesome!" Tristan declared. "Mrs. Greenstreet, NASA
could use your ears. You were fantastic!"

"We should put Rascal back in her cage right now!"
Natalie advised.

"And never let Maria vacuum the landing again," Andi
joked.

Fisher and Will put their heads around the door. "Success?" Fisher asked.

"Success!" Andi announced with satisfaction.

"You guys have been incredible this week," Will said.

"Awesome! As Tristan would say," Mrs. Greenstreet agreed with a laugh.

There was a scrabbling at the door, and Buddy put his nose inside the room. Melissa pulled Rascal tight against her.

"Looks like one of the guests opened the dog-room door after all," Andi sighed. "Come on, Bud. I know you're a Pet Finder, but this is one party you're not invited to!"